SHE
AND 0

by

Kate Rigby

Copyright 2016 Kate Rigby

Cover Design: Based on an Original Image 'Sad Little Girl'
© Marina Dyakonova, Dreamstime.com

This book is licensed for your personal enjoyment only. This book may not be re-sold or given away to other people. If you would like to share this book with another person, please purchase an additional copy for each recipient. If you're reading this book and did not purchase it, or it was not purchased for your use only, then please return to Amazon and purchase your own copy. Thank you for respecting the hard work of this author.

All characters are fictional, and any resemblance to anyone living or dead is accidental

For Tess

Heartfelt thanks to my family and friends for all their encouragement and support.

FOREWORD

This collection of short stories is a similar version to the updated e-book *Tales By Kindlelight*, which I first published a few years ago. The main difference is in the two longer stories: *She Looks Pale* and *Our Marie*. Originally these were one story but for some reason they worked better as standalones, so I cleft them. *She Looks Pale* is available in its own right as an e-book. I thought it would work well, too, fronting a paperback collection of short stories. *Our Marie*, on the other hand, is only included in *Tales By Kindlelight*.

All the stories in both the e-book and the paperback were penned between the turn of the century and 2010 or thereabouts. Some of the inclusions have perhaps already become dated, like *A Generation Thing*, relying as it does on very specific generational differences between the teenaged narrator and her parents of that time. Some of the language and references date it – we know that the narrator is born in 1984, aged eighteen and that the year, therefore, must be 2002. A time before the world of social media as we know it today. The mini piece *Recipe For a Shortened Term in Office* now bears all the hallmarks of sleaze that invaded politics at the time of writing. *Big Mother* is, perhaps, on the cusp of becoming dated, having started out as a satire of Big Brother in its heyday. Although at the time of writing the programme is still being aired, albeit on Channel 5, it has now become a jaded shadow of what it was, devoid of any new ideas, and will surely be axed before too long. The forty-nine-year-old Love Consultant in *Headboards* employs the old fashioned method of placing a newspaper ad rather than all the myriad online ways that have now replaced it and yet I hope the thrust of the story (if you will excuse the pun) is more timeless.

There may be the other occasional reference, coming to the end of its use-by-date, but I hope most other stories stand the test of time, even those with retro references.

Several of the stories have previously been published, before appearing in the e-book *Tales By Kindlelight.* Several were published in various anthologies of avant-garde fiction produced by Skrev Press including: *To The Wire* (2004), *Heads Or Tails* (2005), and *Headboards* and *Cutting Edge* (2006). *Heads Or Tails* has since been renamed *Sharing Sarah.* The risqué short story *Headboards* was also published in an anthology of erotic short fiction *Dancing In The Dark,* published by Pfoxmoor (2011). *The Suit* was first published in Scriptor, Green Arrow Publishing (2004).

A Generation Thing was longlisted for the Fish Short Story Competition (2002) and *Coats* reached the top 50 in the same competition that year.

Both this version and the updated e-book collection include *Biscuits* as a bonus story, which is in fact the 'lost' chapter from my novel *Sucka!* first published by Skrev Press (2004) and now complete with the *Biscuits* chapter in the e-book, renamed *Suckers n Scallies.*

This bittersweet collection, reflects themes for our time, be it the angst of reaching fifty and a life not fully realized, to emerging sexuality or sexual experimentation. In some stories, patterns of behaviour across generations or within a lifetime are explored while other stories look at life from unusual viewpoints. One way or another, I hope something will resonate with you.

Kate Rigby, 2016

CONTENTS

SHE LOOKS PALE	11
COATS	39
CUTTING EDGE	47
SHARING SARAH	57
ON REACHING YOUR HALF CENTURY	67
BOO	73
FAMILY TRADITION	79
AN ANGEL AT MY DOOR	91
GOD ONLINE	99
TO THE WIRE	107
BIG MOTHER	119
STARS	125
KARMIC BREW	135
HEADBOARDS	147
RECIPE FOR A SHORTENED TERM IN OFFICE	159

THE SUIT	**161**
THE COLOUR OF FLESH	**167**
A GENERATION THING	**177**
BISCUITS	**181**

SHE LOOKS PALE

Today is a yellow day. I don't like yellow days. Mother says I won't get hurt in here. I still have my books. Lots of books that take me places. I am taken to the jungle with the tigers where it is hot and yellow. But sometimes I don't want to read any more, so I lie back. *This is the art of levitation, mystery and imagination.* That's what I say when I lie back. Mother told me she used to do it with her friends at Waterloo Park Grammar School. There would be one girl lying on the teacher's table during break and all the other girls in a ring around her, each with two fingers under a part of her body: shoulders, ribs, thighs, ankles. The girl on the table would have her eyes shut and then one girl would start off with: *This is the art of levitation, mystery and imagination. She looks pale, she looks pale, she looks pale.* Each girl had a turn saying it. Auntie Ruth was one of those girls. Auntie Ruth, my father's sister who lives in Amsterdam. She is pale, she is pale, she is pale.

That's what mother always said when I came home from school. She said I was getting paler and paler. Then she said the next chant. She looks ill, she looks ill. Every day mother said it. And then one day I came home with a fearsome headache. I was burning up like the jungle. *She is ill, she is ill*. Mother phoned for an ambulance but she didn't wait for it to come. She bundled me into father's car, and father roared along, but he got caught in a tangle of traffic, and so they got out and ran the rest of the way on foot. Mother was carrying me, bumping me along, but it was scorching and I could see leprechauns. When I woke up in hospital, Doctor Maslen said it was a virus. Mother said it was a Meningitis Scare.

Every day mother says, "I love you. I'll look after you."

First it was the television. We're paying for this, father said to mother one day. We're paying for all this corruption, day in, day out, and look at Hannah sitting there, as if nothing's wrong. It's so subtle. She doesn't flinch when one man pulls a knife on the other. She doesn't hide her face when he pours with blood. She's desensitized already, at the age of eight. Sweet Jesus!

And he pulled out the plug. Then he went to his tools and took out a screwdriver and unscrewed the plug from the flex.

Hot tears fell.

Father said it was for my own good and mother said she'd take me down to the library and get me lots of good books to read, like she used to read when she was a girl. *Famous Five. Secret Seven.* How did that sound?

And then after the Easter holidays there was a new girl in our class called Heather Ferns. She had lovely hair, it was long and dark, and everyone liked her, everyone wanted to be her friend, but she didn't have one special friend to begin with. She'd go round with Stacey, then Kelly, then Emily, but then she was my friend. My best friend, Heather Ferns. Terrible Twins. Heather and Hannah. "We don't have a telly either," she said. "Dad says we can't afford the license fee." And so we played together in our garden, we played with next-door's cat which Heather said was a funny ossity with his funny miaow. We got books out of the library together and mother said it's nice to have a best friend. Mother said her best friend used to live next-door. I have hardly seen mother's best friend but her best friend's mother still lives there. She's called Mrs Cody. I hardly see her either.

Next it was the telephone. We've just sat down to eat, father said one day, and there it goes again, the wretched thing. Always ringing. It's a curse of modern day living. People always trying to get hold of you. People always trying to sell you something. You can never have sanctuary from the outside world because of the wretched telephone and it's getting worse. Chat lines and premium rate numbers. What's the world coming to?

You could get an answerphone, father, I said, shaking the pepper on my casserole, and he said, You see? My nine-year-old daughter advises me to get an answerphone! Why, pray? Why would I want an answerphone? Sweet Jesus. And after the answerphone comes the mobile phone, he said. Mobile phones springing up everywhere. More and more of them. Children as young as Hannah will be asking for them next. You'll see. It's the slippery slope, he said, and pulled out the phone socket. We'll tell BT in the morning, he said to mother. We'll pay what's owing and that'll be that. In fact, we'll write to them. Then they won't try and change our minds which they've all been trained to do. Mother agreed. She said, Whatever's happened to the art of letter-writing?

And after the mobile comes the Internet, father went on. Sweet Jesus, all that filth. How can we protect our daughter? You think they're safe at home between four walls and then that. Pumped into their bedrooms. And he unplugged the computer and wound the flex round and round. Then he put it in a cardboard box. We won't sell it, he said. That's just passing the buck. Spreading it like a virus. Like the Meningitis that might have killed Hannah. We will store it in the loft instead where it'll gather dust or maybe we will burn it. We will burn it on the bonfire because fire purifies.

I didn't tell mother and father about the computers at

my school. But when I went to school the next day, I had other things on my mind because Heather Ferns told me she was leaving our school in the middle of June. I asked her for her new address so we could write to each other and she said she would as soon as she had one. It's important to keep in touch with real friends. Mother kept in touch with her best friend from school for ages.

When I told mother about Heather Ferns leaving school, she said, We got Floaters in my day too, Hannah. She said Floaters can't get attached to one person and when I asked her why, she said it was because they moved from school to school.

Stick to Loyals, Hannah, and you won't go wrong.

So I started playing with Stacey and Kelly. I came home saying everything was cool, and I said shit once when I dropped the carrots on the floor. Mother shook her head and said, School isn't what it was. And father ordered me to my room. I heard him say to mother, I said this would happen. I said that if she goes to school she will make friends, and if she makes friends she will pick up their bad habits and foul language. We need to keep an eye on the sort of friends she mixes with. But we can't when she's at school. We will take her out of school. We will teach her at home.

We used to work flexitime, mother says.

From my bedroom window I can see drifts of blue appearing through the clouds. Dutchman's trousers, mother calls them, and I can hear the buzz of a strimmer. It must be summer.

When was that, mother?

When I worked in an office, she says. Years ago. I'd heard there were jobs going at the rates office where my old school friend Marie was working.

I try and picture mother in her office with its beautiful

electric lights, like great bright bars, warming the ceiling.

It is easy to picture flexitime. I picture it stretching and stretching, like the rubber bands cutting into the piles of papers around the house. Stretching until they snap.

But how does four o'clock become six o'clock? How does light become dark?

Mother tells me that the thinking behind flexitime was to stagger the working day. To make it more flexible. So, for instance, she says, employees could arrive at work any time between 8 o'clock and 10 o'clock, and go home any time between 4 o'clock and 6 o'clock. That way, they could save up several hours until they had enough to take a whole day off. I picture the saved hours, all shiny and stacked together, like 50 pences inside a piggy bank. Or if they wanted to work a shorter day, she says, they would have to pay back the time they owed at a later date. But people tended to stick to their set times, she says. She tells me that she was a 10 till 6-er. (Mother likes categories). All the dirty stop-outs rolled into work at 10 o'clock, she says, but at least I didn't knock off at 4, Hannah. Those people were the laziest shirkers, the 10 till 4-ers. Then you got the run-of-the-mill lot who did 8.30 to 5.30, with one hour for lunch, though some people fiddled their time sheets, Hannah. They'd spend two hours in the pub and if their supervisor wasn't there when they returned, they'd make out as if they'd only taken one hour, or even half an hour. That was Marie, she says, and then there were the ones who worked 8 till 4 because they wanted to go home early, especially in the summer, and there were the 8 to 6 people who took half hour lunches but they weren't all sycophants. Some of the 8 till 6-ers were building up their flexitime so they could take a holiday, Hannah. It was like time off in lieu. TOIL for short. Or Time Off In The Loo, as Marie used to call it.

I can't imagine days packed with different hours any more: one hour painting pictures, one hour playing in the playground, one hour watching children's telly after school.

Mother says, Are you learning anything new, Hannah? This is Social History brought alive. Your mother's life before you were born.

But I used to be able to divide things up, Hannah. Time, space, people. There were always boundaries. Because I was ordered, until I was disordered.

THE PLUG

Once upon a time, there was a boy called Sid. When it got to half past eight in the evening, his mother always said to him, "Sid. It's bath time." Then one day when he was big enough Sid said he would run the bath by himself which he did but he didn't get into the bath. He sat on the side of the bath for twenty minutes, staring into the water now and again, and washing his hands in it so the water would look a bit grey. Then he would get into his night things and say, "Goodnight, mother. Goodnight, father." He always left the plug in. At first his parents thought he'd just forgotten to take the plug out, and then one day his mother said, "Sid. Your neck's still dirty. There's a big tide mark at the back here." Sid said, "I must have missed that bit," and then his mother saw his dirty knees and legs. "You haven't had a bath, Sid, have you?" she said, and he shook his head. "No," he said. "And I'm not having one, ever ever again." His mother didn't know what to do. His father stripped the old chipped cream tiles and put in nice new ones with a Greek motif just like on the Greek vases downstairs which was Sid's favourite motif. His mother started buying nice things to put in the bathroom. She bought a new peach sponge which had airy holes in just like the orange mousses she made which Sid loved. She bought fruity shower gels. Every day she would run the bath and every day Sid would lock the door behind him and sit on the side of the bath in his school uniform, staring at the water as it cooled down. Then he would walk out of the bathroom, leaving the water in the bath untouched. One day, instead of just sitting and staring at the steam rising from the bath, he decided to take off his tie. He rolled it up and placed it on the toilet seat. Then he unbuttoned his shirt and slung it on the towel rail. But he couldn't go any further. So he turned round to the washbasin and washed his hands and face there instead. The basin was all right. The next day he did the same with his tie and his shirt. Then he took off his vest and his trousers, until he was standing there in just his pants and socks. He was shaking. "I can't do it," he thought, and so he washed his hands and face and his neck in the washbasin again. The next day came and he took off all the things he'd taken off before. Then he took off his pants and socks so that he had nothing on. He looked at the water. He held one foot over the water, and then plunged it in. The water was scalding so he took his foot out again and added some cold water. Then he put his foot in again, and the other foot, and did a little dance until his feet got used to the heat. He lowered himself and sat down inside the bath, and he could hear his parents outside the door saying, "I think he's in there. Sid's in the bath." Sid was OK as long as he kept the plug in. Every night he did the same but he climbed out of the bath and let his mother pull the plug out when he was safely out of the bathroom. "Put the plug back in when you've ran the water away," he would ask his mother. At first when he had his baths he would sit at the far end with his chin resting on his knees, as far away from the plug as he could. After a few weeks, he started to relax a bit more in the bath, and he put the plug to the back of his mind. One day he lay back, sponging down his legs, it was like rubbing out grey pencil, and while he did that he tried to think up a song because he liked making up songs. The water around him was like thick scummy broth so that when he put his leg back down he couldn't see it. The plug chain got caught between two of his toes and he could hear the water snoring away down the plughole. He froze. He'd taken his mind off the plug for a few seconds and now look what had happened. He went mad trying to get the plug back in but he couldn't see it through all the grime, and the water was speeding away. The water was nearly gone. He felt the blast of air. It was too late. The fingers were coming. He could see the first one, all big and pointed. Then the other. Then the whole hand. The hand was grabbing at his heel. It was pulling him further and further down until there was just his own hand reaching up the plughole and his distant voice crying "help me, help me".

It is just mother and me. Father left.

Out there, is a wicked land, father said to mother one day. A filthy, disgusting place. It's no place for children because they'll be corrupted as soon as they step out of the front door. There's no innocent hopscotch any more. No shops closed on Sundays. You only have to open a newspaper, he said (when we still took newspapers.) You only have to open it and you will read about children as young as eleven and twelve, mugging and stealing. You will read about them milking their parents dry and demanding the latest computer fad or craze, but it's not the children's fault. It's not even the parents' fault. It's the media. The big companies. The advertisers. The multi-nationals. You will read about children as young as eleven using drugs. Drugs like Ecstasy. Children being made to swallow away their innocence via something as innocuous-looking as a sweet but whose consequences are far from ecstatic. You will read about children as young as eleven, experimenting with their bodies, experimenting with each other's bodies, like adults married for several years. But it is not their fault. They have been brainwashed by years of pop music, pop culture, TV programmes, teen magazines. You will read about children killing each other because the moral fibre of the land is threadbare. And I cannot stand idly by. I cannot bear it that Hannah should inherit such a place. I cannot have it on my conscience any more. Sweet Jesus.

Look after her, Andrea. Promise me you'll carry on protecting her from all evil.

Mother promised.

Then father drank a glass of red wine with his food.

Then he took his serviette from his collar and told us to close our eyes and put our hands together in prayer. *Our Father, which art in heaven, hallowed be thy name ...*

Don't open your eyes, Hannah, until your mother says. Just carry on saying The Lord's Prayer.

Thy kingdom come, thy will be done...

I felt his lips on my forehead, like damp leaves. When I'd finished saying, Forever and Ever Amen, I opened my eyes, and he was gone.

Forever and Ever Amen.

Pink morning clouds puff up behind next-door's chimney pots. A big crow sits on one of them and a row of skinny birds tweet away on the TV aerial. Our house used to be like next-door's with a TV aerial for birds to tweet on. Mother's old school friend used to live next-door. Mother's friend, Marie, who wrote in mother's autograph book at school. She wrote, *If all the swimmers lived over the sea, what a good swimmer Andrea would be.* She wrote it on a yellow page with a blue fountain pen, in handwriting that looks a lot bigger than mother's used to when she was at school.

We went inside next-door's house once, mother and I, when I was little and still going to school. Marie wasn't there but Marie's mother and father were there. "Say please and thank you to Mrs Cody," mother told me. Mother kept hold of me the whole time and I looked up into their light bulb and read the writing. 100 watts. There was a girl in my class called Emily Watts. I wondered if her family made the light bulbs.

When I got home I looked up into our light bulbs. The one in the front room said 60 watts. The ones in the upstairs hall and the downstairs hall said 40 watts. I stared up into the clover of yellow light and then blinked pink clover all over the pale green walls. "Why can't we have 100 watts, father?"

Father frowned. "Envy is a great sin, Hannah."

Mother said, "Economy is a great virtue, Hannah."

Now things are dimmer. 40 watts is the brightest light we have, mother and I. She looks pale, she looks pale. Or we have no light bulbs at all. Just the bare sockets. We have the oil lamps. Mother says that electricity is the root of all evil, just like father said, though before he became frugal, father buzzed like electricity in the sales world, it is said, making lots of money, so that there was plenty in his and mother's joint account when he did his lowly work in the community for several years before he left us.

Maybe he has met up with Emily Watts.

When I stopped going to school, I was allowed one friend to come here and play with me. Emily Watts. Mother vetted her. Her father was a preacher (he didn't make light bulbs after all) and he'd followed my father's example by taking Emily out of school. Mr Watts taught us at home for a while. But then he got a calling to go to Cornwall, and the Watts family left Liverpool. They left Liverpool in a car but the car crashed and they never made it to Cornwall.

It's a sign," father said. "A sign for us to give up the car."

The other day I saw a girl playing in next-door's garden. She was a bit older than me. She was crouching down and shuffling her hands through the stones in the pretty pebble garden that Mr Cody made for Mrs Cody.

The girl's hair was the colour of brown bread. It was tied back but strands of it fell over her wide flat face. I wiped the bedroom window so that I could see all her colours more clearly. Except the muck was on the outside of the window. The girl was wearing pink leggings. Then I heard Mrs Cody's broad accent. "Gemma, love, is Tiddles out there?" Gemma said, "yeah, Auntie Madge, he is," and she picked up the Funny Ossity so his back legs were dangling out in front of him all awkwardly.

I wanted to go out and play with Gemma and Tiddles, like Heather Ferns and I used to do. I tried opening my window but it hadn't been opened for such a long time and by the time I'd loosened the catch, Gemma had gone inside.

I waited for her to come out again but it started raining. I watched the pebbles in Mr Cody's garden go dark and shiny. I watched the clothes on the washing line spot with rain, and I heard Mrs Cody shouting, "Doug, the washing!" and then Mr Cody came out and unpegged the washing from the washing line and put the pegs back in the peg-bag and hugged all the washing in his arms.

Mr Cody said, "You stay right there, Madge. You

know you're not supposed to do too much after your operation."

I wondered what Mrs Cody had been in hospital for. Maybe she would have to stay indoors too in case of the bugs.

I watched the pebbles until they were blown dry and then they turned bright and pale with a flash of sun over them.

She looks pale, she looks pale

I waited for Gemma but she didn't come out to play again that day.

Today is a rainbow day. I like rainbow days. They make me think of Auntie Ruth. I was dreaming about Auntie Ruth before. She was wearing a gown like headmasters used to wear, only hers was bright lime with big black spots, and in her arms she held a pussy cat. It was the cat from next-door, the Funny Ossity.

I only ever saw Auntie Ruth that time after my Meningitis Scare. She came back from Holland with Uncle Rick and they stayed with an old friend of Auntie Ruth's in Litherland.

I opened my eyes in hospital and there were all these lovely colours. Her hair was purple like a thistle and her jumper was full of vivid flecks. I could feel the blissful cool of her rings and bracelets as she held my hand, anchoring me back into the world. In her other hand she had two bags: a small bulging brown paper bag and a smooth shiny white plastic bag with a fancy logo.

"There's fruit in that one, Hannah," she said, about the paper bag. "Grapes and cherries."

Then she slid me the large glossy bag. "Well? Open it."

I dipped in and pulled out a pink cardigan, soft and fluffy as a kitten. I couldn't take my eyes off it. It was my favourite colour. The best cardigan I'd ever owned. I put it against my cheek and purred.

"Look, mother. Look what Auntie Ruth gave me."

But mother didn't feel the same about it. "I'm surprised at Auntie Ruth," she said, even though Auntie Ruth was one of mother's closest friends at school. "It's a bit garish, Hannah. Distasteful. Taste is something that comes with age."

So it got whisked away to the back of mother's wardrobe but she promised me we would go shopping to buy a nice new dress for me. I tried to look pleased, otherwise I would miss out on the dress as well, so when we went to the dress shop I made a beeline for the lime dress with black spots on, big as bumble bees.

"I like *that* dress, mother. Which one do you like?"

"One that's more subtle, Hannah," she said, her frantic fingers working down the rail until they landed on something. She pulled it out. "Like this one."

I stared at this one. It was the colour of dead leaves and dried turds.

Mother and father came to live in this house after grandma died. Grandma Lafferty, who died before I was born. In her photographs, Grandma looks proud and navy-blue. I don't think she had any clothes in any other colours. Maybe Grandma only wore navy-blue when she was having her picture taken, like I used to for school photographs, dressed in my uniform, all neatly ironed, when mother used to be thorough about ironing. So thorough that I could smell the scorching on my school blouse and feel the hot collar against my neck.

I think about the old photographs in the cupboard under the stairs, and while mother reads and marks my work, THE PLUG, I creep down to the box under the stairs and pull out one of the albums. It's one of those with sticky flaps that you peel back from the pictures like cling film. On the first page there is mother in her school uniform: a pale blue jumper and navy blue skirt. *All in blue, all in blue.* A fragment of a tune I'd overhear mother singing when she was glowing with wine. An echo from the past that wafted up through the floorboards, through my pillow. *All in blue, all in blue, she said the baby's due.* In the picture, mother's hair is tied back so tight I can feel it hurting and she looks pale, she looks pale. Sometimes Grandma Lafferty kept her off school because she looked pale. Above the photograph there is writing. *Waterloo Park 1971.* I turn the page and there is mother again, in her summer uniform which is a white flower print on a turquoise background. She is standing next to her friend who has her hand over mother's head, like an octopus. They have clumpy wet-look shoes on their feet. Mother told me they were all the rage at the time, those wet-look shoes. *Me and Marie 1972.* Over the page mother's dressed up to go out, with lavender-blue eyeshadow and her hair tightly curled. There's an artificial blush on her cheeks. *Me in smock and loon pants – Emancipation Dance 1972.* I turn the pages. Mother is getting older and shapelier, her hair shorter and yellower. Like a chick's. Marie has dark hair and fair skin and mischievous blue eyes. There's a picture of Marie holding on to a man with permed hair. The man's wearing big flared trousers that have a high waistband with three buttons on it. On top he's wearing a jacket with big lapels and only one button as big as an old penny. *Marie and Gareth 1976.* I turn more pages. There are several shots of a crowd of heads, probably taken in poor light because the brightest thing in each picture is a blue globe of light in the foreground. Like a blue oil lamp. *Candlelit vigil for John Lennon, St George's Hall, December 1980.* I try and imagine which of those heads are my mother's and father's, and which ones might be Marie and the man that asked her to marry him on the way home. Marie said yes to his proposal, but mother told me that the marriage didn't last long because Marie didn't take her vows seriously. Mother had a fall out with Marie over it. Loyalty is everything, Hannah, she said.

I turn more pages and there are some pictures of mother and father with red-eye and always holding glasses of wine or beer, until the nineteen-nineties when their photographs get more and more sober. I start appearing on a few, though there are other albums somewhere, dedicated just to me. But this album looks like odds and ends, where I just slipped in with a blurred arm or a fuzzy face, and then there are no more pictures except the ones in my head.

Mother finds me. She has my story book in her hand. She can see I'm getting stuck into Social History which is a favourite of hers. She has marked my story THE PLUG. She has given me a B+ and after the grade she's written in tiny red handwriting: *Sid is right to be afraid of plugholes and has personified the bacteria lurking therein.*

Mother is seventeen. She's taking a half-day off, flexitime. Mother's been saving it up, her flexitime, like her money which she wants to spend in town this afternoon. It is a hot greasy day in August. It's been a greasy summer. There's a drought on, up and down the country. She gets the bus into town where she buys a bottle of Chantilly perfume which smells as sweet as flowers, and a dress from Justin, and a skirt the colour of a peeled potato from Chelsea Girl.

She doesn't know what to wear tonight. Marie says if mother wears the black dress, she'll have to wear a dark bra under it because the ultraviolet lights will pick out a white bra like an X-ray. When I went to hospital when I was a little girl, did I have an X-ray? Did they look inside my head and see my Suspected Meningitis? Mother tries on her peeled potato skirt but worries that everyone will be able to see her legs through it because the material is flimsy. On top she wears her halter neck but it's black too and mother says the ultraviolet lights will pick out all the fluff on it, however much she brushes it down with the clothes brush first. I have seen those ultraviolet lights. I went to a disco when I was seven years old. Kelly and Stacey were there and we all danced together. The lights showed all the freckles on Kelly's face, and her teeth and eyes were like glow stars. So were Stacey's. We all pointed and giggled at each other's funny teeth and eyes and all the fluff like snow on our shoulders. Mother sat near me the whole time, I felt her ultraviolet eyes watching me, and then she checked her watch and went to find father who took us home.

Mother likes going to the nightclub with Marie. Mother met father in a nightclub too. The lights made his skin look bronze, like he'd been to the Bahamas for two weeks, and his eyes looked a brilliant blue. He looked as if the colour might need adjusting, or the contrast, mother said, and it was strange for her to see him in the daylight. But she knew what he looked like in the daylight because he was her school friend's older brother. Her school friend, Ruth.

But mother hasn't met father in that way yet. She just goes to the nightclubs and enjoys herself with Marie. Marie gives her fun and freedom, I read it in her diary. DESK DIARY 1976. *Oh that girl! The fun and freedom I have with her! She brings out another side of me for sure! The wicked drinking side. I don't really remember much about last night. Just trailers.*

I think I spent half of last night bending over the loo, or reading the graffiti. WHY DOES THE POPE WEAR UNDERPANTS IN THE BATH? SO HE DOESN'T HAVE TO LOOK DOWN ON THE UNEMPLOYED. I fixed it in my head. That's the sort of joke I want to remember to tell others. Then I must have come out on to the dance floor because I remember some fella saying to me, "Is that the shanty town look?" God, I must have looked rough, and then all I remember is that we were outside in the street, trying to flag down a cab in Hanover Street. "I've got to get home, Marie. I've got to get home." Even though I was palatic, I was thinking of mum worrying about me, so we flagged down a cab which wasn't a cab. The light was just a torch on his dashboard but I didn't notice till we were half way home. He could have been anyone, though he seemed a friendly enough fella, what I remember of him, which isn't much, though Marie said he was a BOA. (Bit Of Alright).

And we were singing a song we used to sing in school. That one Marie taught everyone. And it's still going round in my head.

*All in fawn, all in fawn, she said the baby's born
Down the back alley where nobody goes*

I've heard that song somewhere. Deep down I know it. It comes to me in echoes, in pieces, from years ago, from the time before my Meningitis Scare.

One day I looked through the spirals of spiders' webs on the window to the garden where mother was digging a great big hole. I watched her heel forcing the spade into the earth until it held a full load which she chucked behind the trench with the rest. She was wearing green wellingtons, a skirt and an anorak. She had smears of mud on her face which was bright poppy like my Meningitis Face.

She was planting something. Maybe it was potatoes. Maybe it was a little tree which would grow a foot each year so that by the time I was twenty it would be towering over me. But no tree has ever come up there.

Mother closed the hole and raked over it. Mother is strong for one so slight. She has never liked physical work. "Exercise makes me dizzy," she often says. "Fielding in rounders was about my limit. On third post. Even then, I sometimes had to run after the ball if Beverley Hall slogged it as far as the nettles. Then it would be my fault if the batting team won because I couldn't run fast enough."

I thought about going out to help mother in the garden. I thought it might halve her dizziness if she had someone to help her, and it would have been fun to do some gardening anyway. Then I looked over to mother's left, to the black patch on the lawn, all charred. I squinted my eyes, wondering how long it would take for the grass to grow green again, and suddenly mother was standing behind me.

Was it a bonfire, mother? Did I miss it?

You were fast asleep, Hannah. And sleep is so important for your health. It wasn't for fun, Hannah. All the dead branches and stalks needed burning away. That's all.

Are you still planting, mother? Can I come out and help you in the garden?

Years ago, there used to be redwings, she said. Redwings and yellowhammers and greenfinches. You never see them any more. The garden isn't what it used to be, believe me, Hannah. The garden is no place for you. It is full of dirt and bacteria, maybe even the bacteria that nearly killed you when you were a little girl.

What if you were to cut yourself on a rusty nail? I would never forgive myself, Hannah. There are too many dangers lurking out there.

I promised your father, Hannah. He is watching over us. He is in another land, Hannah. Another dimension, where there is no bacteria, no super bugs, just everlasting life.

I think I know that place. It's the place of mystery and imagination where you go after the art of levitation. You rise and rise through the vapours, through the clouds, and then you are there.

There are white plumes coming from the chimney opposite and all the roof tiles are frosty white but the sky is heavy, like a headache. Perhaps it will snow. I dreamt of snow earlier. Pink snow. It looked heavenly, like tufts of pink mohair that would join into one big cardigan on the ground, like the one Auntie Ruth gave me in hospital after my Meningitis Scare.

But I'm not looking at the sick clouds now, *she looks ill, she looks ill,* because I can see them playing in next-door's garden. Gemma and her younger sister and little brother. Gemma's nose is red and she's got red tinsel in her hair. All in red, all in red. I think it might be Christmas Day or Boxing Day or one of those days around Christmas because they've got Christmas lights in their window which look beautiful. I watch them twinkle through the chink in my curtain after dark, remembering the taste of walnuts, scooped out like dried brains from shells cracked open with nutcrackers.

I said to mother the other day, Is it Christmas soon?

Christmas? she said. Do you think so, Hannah? Do you really think so?

Then she said, We will light a candle for the baby Jesus, shall we, Hannah? Shall we?

Will we give presents to each other, mother?

Presents? she said. Oh I don't think so, Hannah. I don't think so. What would we give? We have nothing but each other.

Will we give cards then, mother?

Her eyes steamed up, and then she told me about cards. She used to buy an assortment, and then put them in piles according to design. Because mother likes categories. Sedate trees and snow scenes for the old folk. Doves of peace and nice cards for best friends, for people she really cared about. The medium cards for more distant friends. Then there were the cards that got left at the bottom of the box. The ones with candles and baubles and sentimental rhymes. They were for acquaintances and people at work who you had to give a card to because they'd given you one. It says a lot about the person who gives that sort of card, she said. And I didn't want to be thought of as a person who hasn't got good taste when it comes to cards, Hannah. Mrs Cody sends those sorts of cards. She buys them in January. Ten for a pound from a tub outside a discount shop, Hannah.

Mother is out at the moment. She rarely goes out. Maybe she's gone to buy some cards with doves of peace on the front. Two of the children next-door are going back indoors. But one of the girls is still out there with the Funny Ossity. The Funny Ossity is on the fence between our gardens. If I pull open my curtains and knock on the window the girl will see me. I don't need to knock. When I move the curtain, it makes her look up. I'm waving but she isn't waving back. She's squinting. Maybe I look faint behind a mucky window which has no electric bulb to light it up. I go downstairs, shuffling through all the sheets of newspaper and junk mail and dead leaves that litter the hall on the way to the back door. The back door is locked. I'm rattling it. Where is the key? Has mother taken it? Do we have a spare? There are keys in the draw by the sink. Here's one, long and clanky with a bit of yellow string tied through it. Slip it into the lock, it fits, it fits! But the old lock isn't budging, not all the way, but enough, enough! The door is opening. The air is fresh and bracing. The Funny Ossity scrambles over our fence. Puss puss, here puss puss. He comes over to sniff my fingers. He must recognize my smell from when Heather and I used to play with him. Heather and Hannah, the Terrible Twins. Then he darts through our back door, when he hears mother trudging up the path. I dash back inside and shut the door but mother is through it before I have time to lock it.

What were you doing, Hannah? What were you doing?

I had a headache, mother. I needed some air.

A headache? Oh no. Oh no. Get upstairs, quickly.

She is ill. She is ill.

See what happens when you open the door, Hannah. You let in the germs, the corruption. All the bad things. But I promised your father. I promised him. Stay in your room, Hannah. We'll lock the door and then you'll be safe in there.

Can I keep the cat, mother? To play with?

Dear Heather,

Do you remember me? Hannah and Heather, the Terrible Twins. I have the Funny Ossity now. I've called him Henry. Funny Ossity Henry. Henry sounds majestic and suits him better than Tiddles, don't you think? He came from next-door but he's decided to stay here. He sits on my bed. I am in bed at the moment because I haven't been well so I have plenty of time to write letters. I can't remember what the date is. Mother says I'm ill–

She is ill, she is ill.

Oh don't get out of bed, Hannah. You have no coordination because you are so ill and weak. The house is full of bugs and I can't keep up with them. Killer bugs. Bacteria. Meningococcalitis. But in your bed, Hannah, it's the safest place to be. I will carry you to the toilet because your legs are weak. The plastic sheeting is just in case you have an accident. You are ill, and I am looking after you. I've stocked up on the Complan. I've got different flavours, Hannah, you won't get bored. The larder is full of Complan, so there's no need to worry, Hannah. Everything is taken care of.

Through the twelve-inch gap between the curtains I can see the bit of window covered in dried splashes and muck and grime. I can see leaves and spiders' webs stuck to the pane.

Today is a yellow day. I don't like yellow days. Mother says I won't get hurt in here. I still have my books. Lots of books that take me places. I am taken to the jungle with the tigers where it is hot and yellow. But sometimes I don't want to read any more so I lie back. *This is the art of levitation, mystery and imagination.* That's what I say when I lie back.

Every day mother tells me she loves me. Her knuckles are red and raw like her eyes. She bites them or chews them, like Henry chews his fur when he's washing himself. I am used to the dim light from the half-closed curtains. I am like Henry. Henry has indoor eyes that shine at night like glow stars. I can hear him crunching on his dry food. But I am safe in my bed, mother says.

And when there are knocks at the front door, mother is quiet as a whisper until they go away. She is afraid of the knocks because afterwards she unlocks my door and sits on my bed and chews her knuckles. I won't let them take you, she says. I won't let them take you. She feels like bones when she hugs me.

Henry limps after a mouse as it scampers through the unopened letters on the floor. Sometimes mother comes in with a pile of letters in her hand. Then she'll put the letters down and forget about them. There's one just down below me. If I wiggle my hand I'll be able to reach it. There. Got it. Which is more than Henry's done with the mouse. The letter's addressed to mother. *Mrs A Alleway.* It's got a postmark. *Dorset and SW Hants.* I wonder who mother knows all the way down there. And at the top it says, *Please forward.* It isn't a bill because it's handwritten. I will open it because it might be important. Mother never opens anything any more. She says there are germs where people have licked the gum flaps.

Page 3. I remember when I thought white tights were the last word in fashion. I wanted some because Bev Hall had some. Remember that time she beat me up in the playground cause I'd snogged Keith whatshisface at the Emancipation Dance? Emancipation Dances! Frigging hell! They were pushing back the frontiers in their day. I can remember the smock I was wearing: cream cheesecloth over maroon loons. Jesus, those loons. I bought them in Cape for £2 and then tried to fray the bottoms. You had on a smock and loons too that night, I remember, clear as if it was yesterday. Yeah, I remember seeing you and thinking, God, she looks good out of her uniform (Page 4) with her hair curled and in make-up and that. Remember when we did all that levitation stuff? She looks ill, shizzle! Me and Ruth used to be in bulk when it got to the shizzle bit. Do you ever see anything of your sister-in-law? That was some cult, wasn't it, that they grew up in, her and David. Those long plaits of hers. And no pop music or telly or mates over for tea. What a life. Plymouth Brethren, that was it. But she was always up for a laugh. Her and David. They managed to break free, didn't they? Are you and David still together? How's your daughter? Mum thinks you might have moved or that you and David might have split up. She's not seen or heard anything from you. I've made such a mess of things. I keep thinking back to my wedding day all those years ago (page 5) and how everyone said what a lovely couple we made at the wedding, and Mike was a nice fella, but not to live with

As for babies, well. You were braver than me on that score. I've never wanted all that pain. Oh but I'm sorry I've not been much of a mate these past few years, Andie, but I do think about you, and the fun we had clubbing. Was it 76? All that dancing and all our codes. Remember? BOA (Bit of Alright) and AOT (After One Thing). Jesus, I couldn't do it now. Coming home at three in the morning and wanting to murder a bacon sarnie and wiping all that muck off my face. But those years have a smell about them. The perfumes. Chanel no 5 and that Chantilly perfume. Was that yours or mine? I can't remember. A lot of it's completely obliterated by all that Cherry B and Cider, and Babycham, and Pony. Pony! God in heaven, that was disgusting stuff, wasn't it?

And I always remember your groups, Andie. The Droppers and the Loyals. (Page 6) I remember you telling me I was a Loyal like you and I thought that was a good thing to be. Did you have a group called the Schemers? For those who plot behind your back? You were ahead of yourself, that's for sure. I've been putting my mates in these categories ever since. I know I haven't been much of a Loyal to you. I thought my life was about

Loyals but it's been more about Droppers lately. Maybe you think I'm a Dropper now but it's not too late, Andie, to pick up where we left off–

Maybe I could write to Marie, Henry. Marie is to mum as Heather was to me. I could write to her and tell her that mother and I are Loyals and that we need to see her soon, and we would be happy for her to pick up where she left off. I have her address here. I could tell mother what I'm doing but then she'd know I'd opened her private letter with the germs on the gum flap but if I don't tell her, how will I get it posted? Unless I dropped it out of the window into Mrs Cody's garden but even if I could fight my way out of my bed, the window is a whole obstacle course away and such a pain to open.

Unless you took it, Henry. Unless you carry it in your mouth like a mouse and I am slipping into sleep, dreaming of Henry with my letter clamped in his jaws...

I am nearly awake. Flies whirr past my ear, but I am still dreaming of the traffic lights rising out of the ocean. All of them flashing amber. *Today is a sick amber day at sea.* Amber is the colour of sickness for sure. People never have a healthy amber glow. I remember father driving me through amber lights on our way to the hospital when I had my Meningitis Scare. Father didn't mind the flashing amber. Flashing amber meant putting his foot down. But he jumped the still amber too. "Bloody traffic lights," he said. "Always against you in an emergency." And so they left the car and mother carried me the rest of the way, through the leprechauns.

Mother comes into the room to comb my hair with the toothbrush. She says, When you have a baby, Hannah, you have to make sure it is alive all the time. You fret, night and day. Has it stopped breathing? Why can't you hear it? That's what it's like being a mother, Hannah. Constantly checking up on your sleeping baby. Life is never the same again. Your mind is never free to wander. Your sleep is never unbroken.

Always on amber alert.

Water pools through the window ledge which is covered in green slime. I can see it through the gap in the curtain. If I could catch it I would drink it. I would drink anything because I am thirsty. Heather once told me that you could drink your own wee. It's perfectly safe, Hannah, she said. My dad told me. He once went on this survival course, she said.

Wee is the colour of amber.

Mother puts up the ironing board and stands the old iron on the metal bit at the end. She irons away on the board, backwards and forwards, as if she's sanding it down, while the Funny Ossity plays with the dangling plug.

I watch the cold iron, moving fast like a motorboat, making all the right movements. I remember the smell as the iron scorched over the collar of my old school blouse. Mother hums, and then, as she's folding away she board, she says, Your father always said it was satisfying coming to the end of something. A bit like a game of cards. If you've played a good hand, of course. You see, Hannah, life is something to get through. Like work.

Like traffic lights.

It is a chore, Hannah. Like ironing.

It is a duty.

And who are we, Hannah?

We are smaller than life. Like the little injured bird, Hannah. The one I tried to save once when I was at school. I kept him in a shoebox, I did all I could for that poor bird, but he gave up on me, he gave up the ghost because he was smaller than life.

But mother will come soon with the baby's bottle. You are my baby, Hannah. You are my sick baby. I felt a clump of her hair. It felt like matting, the same as mine. There are creatures in my hair. I bashed one dead on the pillow, and then I felt sorry for it, seeing it with its legs folded in and lying in a trail of brown juice. *She looks dead, she looks dead.*

Mother, mother, I can't feel my legs. They are cut off from me but in my dreams they walk places.

And after amber comes red. Red for Meningitis. Red for danger. *All in red, all in red, she said the baby's dead.*

Henry does another curl of poo on the floor, his dirt tray is full and crowded with flies. Then he jumps through a parting in the leprechauns and sits on the window sill with a white halo around him. He is doing my speaking for me because my mouth has furred up, and no matter how much I call for mother, the words are just a hoarse rattle in my windpipe along with father's voice. *Not long now, Hannah. Not long.* My windpipe is like the plughole. The plug has been pulled but the bath is empty. And when there's no water left to go down, that's when the hand will come and pull me down.

Oh but mother will come soon, she'll come and lie down with me on the squelchy bed, and together we will say, this is the art of levitation, mystery and imagination …

It is a white day. I'm lying on the table. There they all are. Heather Ferns and Kelly and Stacey and Emily Watts. Each with two fingers under my white robe. Emily is wearing a muslin mask when she starts the ball rolling. This is the art of levitation, mystery and imagination, she looks pale, she looks pale. There's a strong smell of lint and antiseptic, she is pale, she is sickly pale under the bright square light hinged over her, turning her white, ill, she looks ill, very ill, Stacey's voice is ghostly now, ultraviolet, like the rays at the disco, she is ill, very ill, I can feel their fingers beneath me, but I am a feather, I will rise up any minute, watch me, we're losing her, she looks dead, she's rising, the light is getting brighter, I'm rising as high as the hinged light which opens out into a land of white, it is heaven light, coming nearer, she is dead, she is dead, there is father, sweet Jesus, and mother, coming out of the light like an angel, one, two, three, four, you're coming to live with me, Hannah, with us, in our new house, five six, seven, eight, I'm joining myself in the world of mystery and imagination, nine, ten, there's mother's hand, I'm touching it, please don't let go, I haven't quite got hold,

I'm slipping,
I still have hold of the hand,
Auntie Ruth's hand,
And I hear the ring of voices.
She looks brighter, she looks …

COATS

"Coming ready or not, Wendy!"

Peter's voice.

Wendy burrows deep under the heap of coats on Shirley's parents' bed. The grown-ups' singing to Shirley downstairs – *She's got the key of the door, never been twenty-one before* – muffled now through a suffocating pair of duffel coats, smelling of old garages.

This is where all the coats gather for a party of their own: posh coats and lowly coats, soft coats and tough coats, plain coats, fussy coats.

Wendy shuffles about, nudging up to the scent of female coats, sniffing what has to be her big sister's midi. She'd know that sweet orangey scent anywhere. Smells like the Aqua Manda Penny cadged off Shirley's younger sister, Lorraine.

"Found you! Found you!"

Peter makes a parting through the coats and squirms in beside her. "Budge over, Wendy."

Earlier in the year, she and Peter played under the coats when Lorraine Jackson got engaged to Jimmy Walters. Peter tickled her under her poncho, an old one of Penny's which Penny had no further use for, and Wendy giggled lots, tickling him back under his Fair Isle tank top, passed down by his cousin. Then he put his hand over her mouth to shush her when a shard of landing light lit up their hidey-hole.

She could spy some legs – thick legs in python skin boots – through the buttonhole of a large male coat and when she jiggled the buttonhole up a bit she saw black stockings, with ladders in, like tiny skyscrapers. Up some more, and she saw the girl's bosom-banger pushed out over the big cliff of her bust. Size 38C, people said about Buxom Bev Brown, the fishmonger's daughter. Then she saw another pair of legs closing in on Bev as she slid against the wall. Wendy wondered how much Peter could see, though doubtless she had the best view.

"It's you I want, Bev," Jimmy Walters said, hurling his greasy denim jacket towards the bed. It missed and fell on the floor. "Been mentally undressing you all bloody evening."

Buxom Bev started cackling, just like the fishmonger, only higher pitched.

Then Jimmy said, "Now I'm gonna really undress you!"

That's when Buxom Bev gave him a bit of a slap that didn't sound cross at all. "Oy, you'll be getting me a bad reputation, Jimmy Walters. Anyway, what about Lorraine?"

"Bloody frigid. Even now, when we're supposed to be engaged."

"Well, bloody pack her up then."

"I will, baby. I bloody well will."

Jimmy Walters and Buxom Bev got stuck together in a kiss and Bev slipped out of her turquoise wet-look coat which came winging over Wendy's buttonhole like a blackout. Wendy heard the closing and bolting of Shirley Jackson's parents' door, and before long she and Peter were being treated to a seasick ride as the springs went boing boing under the weight of Jimmy and Buxom Bev. She and Peter had to squash up small and hold their lips under the coats on the bed. She pinched Peter when he burped like a frog and he pinched her back when her snuffled giggle threatened to escape, though Buxom Bev was making quite a din herself, panting sounds, like in the 100 metres race. She sounded like a dying duck in a thunderstorm gone wrong, Peter said afterwards, though Wendy suspected it had something to do with the Facts of Life. She knew she'd have to get Penny to fill in the gaps because Peter, younger than her by eighteen months, only had a little sister and the much older boy cousin (ex-owner of the tank top) who she doubted shared those sort of secrets with him.

Bloody pack her up, Buxom Bev told Jimmy at the engagement party but Jimmy and Lorraine Jackson are still going strong. Getting married next year, Penny told Wendy.

"Coats up in our bedroom," comes the bubbly voice of Mrs Jackson, and more coats rain down on Wendy and Peter as the late arrivals come straight from the boozer, Jimmy Walters among them.

Peter snakes his hand up through the pile. "I think this one's Jimmy's," he says, whacking a stiff leather arm against Wendy's cheek.

"Pwooor. It stinks, Peter. Of fags and cider and petrol."

"D'you think Buxom Bev has come tonight, Wendy?"

They rummage through the coats, plucking out likely sleeves of Buxom Bev's – a shiny plastic, a worn denim, a mock leather – their noses ferreting for a coat with a slight whiff of Mr Brown's finest skate.

Mungo Jerry sounds louder as the Jackson parents' door opens wide and more coats come to entomb them. A pair of legs come by the bed, a female's, trailing bog roll under her snakeskin boots as she dumps her coat down, wailing to herself. (Is she drunk?) Wendy briefly sees a stray balloon, one of those long, wiggly, snazzy sorts, popping rudely as the boot heels stagger across it, and then between Mungo Jerry and Ringo Starr she hears the voice of Penny. "Anyone seen Wendy? I bet she's still playing hide and seek with little Peter."

"Little Peter, huh, cheek!"

"Kick the door shut, *Little Peter*, so it's all dark again."

More giggling, as she and Peter spring up, like fountains from the earth. One Two Three, down again. One Two Three, up for air. One Two Three, down again. Diving right down into the coats and holding their breath, like they do in the swimming baths. All they want to do is play: play forever under the coats.

"This man must have got a big big head," Peter says, fishing out a great woolly hat. Peter is a good diver. He hangs the hat on the end of his fist, spinning it around.

"D'you think he's old, Peter?"

"I dunno." He takes a sniff inside. "Ruddy hell! He never washes his hair, that's for sure."

Peter always makes her sides split till she's nearly weeing herself.

They're playing Guess the Coats. She feels another, it's an old person's coat, an old woman's she'd say, you can tell by its smell and the loose button in the pocket. Miss Featherstone's? Except Miss Featherstone wouldn't dump it down in the pool of coats, would she? No, she'd keep it on all evening, knowing Miss Featherstone, while sitting on her favourite hard wooden chair.

Oh there's so much fun to be had up here with the coats: the smells, the shapes, the pockets! Peter's already inside the pockets of what feels like a reefer jacket. "Money, Wendy. Ruddy hell!"

Just think how much they could make if they went through all the pockets.

"Is it lots?" She's squinting for a peek, though it's easier to feel the coins in Peter's moist outstretched palm: two new half pence pieces.

She knows she can do better as she rolls aside a bundled shawl in favour of something more solid. Is it a cape? She bets it's red, like Red Riding Hood's, like Mrs Jackson would wear, or even Shirley Jackson, now that she's twenty-one. It's like Christmas, this delving into pockets in the dark, guessing what's inside, with only shape and texture to help them.

"Look, it's a scarf, Peter!" She whips it free from the cape, like magicians do. It's a chiffon scarf, like Penny used to wear when they were 'in'. She swirls it round her neck as she and Peter fight over the next pocket in the queue – a clammy suede (it feels like) with fringes and ripped lining and so threadbare it's shiny. She wonders who could own such a rag. Maybe Buxom Bev, or Jimmy Walters' sister if he's got one.

"You do the right pocket, Peter. I'll do the left."

"Bingo, Wendy. I've got something."

(Her pocket has a hole in it, right through to the lining). "What is it?"

"Dunno. I think it's a cigarette lighter."

"No, silly. It's a lipstick."

"Dare you to put it on."

"It might be a shitty colour." (They both crease up at the word 'shitty'.)

"D'you think it might be Buxom Bev's?"

Peter takes it off her and she hears the snap of the lid as he pulls the top off, giving it a twizzle until the lipstick is up as far as it'll go. She can see the silhouette of it against the wall. He kneels up, making a tent of some of the coats, and starts crayoning her lips in the dark.

She giggles and then pinches him.

"It's up too far, you twerp. It'll break right off!"

No sooner said as happens, and it's, quick quick, shove the lid back on, shove it back in the pocket, she'll never know. Was it the right pocket or the left? It was yours, the right, mine had a hole in. More fits of laughter. Peter is so close she can smell him. He smells of Liquorice Allsorts. The bobbly blue ones, the ones they fight over. As she laughs her whole body rocks and each time she rocks she feels something flump against her leg, cool and spongy, a bit moist: something that's working its way free from the bundled up shawl.

"Peter. Feel this, here. What is it?"

He scrabbles in vain so she guides his hand to the UO (Unidentified Object).

"Eeer, it feels all slimy, Wendy."

She pictures something from Mr Brown's fishmonger's carried not in the shawl but in Miss Featherstone's bag, netted like a Christmas stocking. She thrusts her nose down towards it, like a cat, sniffing for rotting haddock

Then Peter says, "It feels like a little foot."

She giggles.

"I think it's a baby, Wendy."

"A baby? " More giggles. "Don't be daft."

"Scout's honour," Peter says, leading her hand to the alleged foot, but she pulls it away as if from a hot ring.

"You'd hear crying, Peter."

"Maybe it's asleep."

"Where would it have come from?"

"Perhaps it's a doll, Wendy. They make them look really real nowadays. My sister's got one. Tiny Tears or something. It cries real tears. Here, let me see if it's got a string on its back

"Is there one?"

He gropes about a bit more. "No, but it's got one at the front, down by its belly button. Should I pull it?"

"Should we put the light on, Peter?"

"No, we might wake it. Let's wrap it back up in the shawl and leave it to sleep."

As Peter's folding the shawl around the baby, they hear Penny calling: "Wendy? Peter? Where are you? We're about to do the toast."

They emerge from their secret cave of coats then, turning their heads once for a last squint until the shawl is back as it was, just an ordinary empty shawl, waiting for a mature woman's shoulders to wrap itself around against the cold wind. Then blinking in the hall light, they softly tread the stairs towards *for she's a jolly good fellow, for she's a jolly good fellow...*

CUTTING EDGE

Nanny nicks the air with a few squeaky snips of the scissors before offering them to Hilary. The scissors have rounded ends and Hilary cuts out the chain of Mummies and Daddies that Nanny helped her crayon. Father's fist on the table now becomes only a blurred edge of sound, out of focus, like Mother's sobbing, as Hilary loses herself in the happy paper figures, the way she loses herself in the Happy Families cards. She thinks of the huge bright faces on the cards, imagining herself as Mr Snip, the Tailor. He has scissors too, like the barber where she and Father go to have their hair trimmed. "Short back and sides," Father always says. Hilary remembers her long sturdy plait which the Barber snipped off with one jag of his big scissors. One day there, a rod for her back; the next, just lying there in the Barber's hand like a dead snake. "You can take it home and your mother will put it in an envelope," the Barber said. He was wearing his grey overall and when he'd finished he brushed the back of her neck and the floor felt springy as she walked through small islands of hairs to the till with Father.

Hilary carries on cutting. The scissors go squeak squeak. They get bigger and sharper as her older grammar school fingers hook through them and guide them with perfect dexterity. At the Girl's Grammar her supposed best friend is Frances who is tall and can see over a field of heads, to the Incorrigibles (as Miss Clapham calls them.)

One day Frances dips her pen in her inkwell and whispers to Hilary, "So why did your mother and father get divorced?"

Divorced! Such a shameful word, even to be whispered in public, and Hilary is silent as she copies the list of irregular French verbs from the blackboard. It is forbidden to talk idly in the classroom, thank goodness. It can earn you a rap on the knuckles.

"A mistress, was it?" There's something cutting about Frances' voice as she whistles it through her teeth.

Miss Clapham turns round and glares at her pupils. She won't ask for hush again.

By the time Form 2B are scurrying homewards with their weighty satchels, Frances' stories have grown horns. "Her father? Four prostitutes? I thought he was a pillar of society."

"A pillow of society would be more accurate," the Incorrigibles snigger.

Hilary blinks back tears. It's true that her parents' marriage has been split in two; that Father has left Mother to move in with his mistress, but the other rumours are nothing but nasty fibs.

She hurries home to the decaying house which she and Mother share with its overgrown palm trees outside the bay windows. Father always described the palm trees as vulgar. "I'm home, Mother," she calls, and heads straight for the dining room table where she lays out the new material that Mother bought her for her thirteenth birthday. The fabric smells of the haberdashery in town. She loves that smell. On her birthday she pinned all the pattern pieces to what will become her apron. She now takes out the scissors from Mother's sewing basket (which used to belong to Grandmother) and hears the satisfying echo of the blades against the table as they cut around the pattern. Nothing matters but that hollow slicing sound.

She cuts out more patterns on the dining room table,

where Father doesn't sit any more, until she no longer needs patterns.

She carefully cuts through the years and when she is eighteen, gets her first job in a hairdressing salon. (It was a choice between that or dressmaking.) Her first ever proper customer is a young man. She's never done a man's hair before. All her supervised cuts were on ladies of advancing years. The man has sharp points to his face and a metallic glint in his eye which she finds appealing. She'd like to style his hair like Elvis Presley's. With a jagged quiff.

The man smiles at her through the mirror.

"I do like a lady to do my hair."

She blushes as she takes a section of his hair and uses a wide-toothed comb through it. They say every hairdresser remembers her first cut. Her first proper, unsupervised cut.

"You're my first ever," she tells him which causes her boss Mrs Willoughby to do a lot of ahem-ing until she is forced to leave her young man and join Mrs Willoughby in the corner over the brush they use to sweep up.

"Don't let them know they're your first, Miss Kent," Mrs Willoughby says, resorting to her admonishing tone. "It'll make them nervous."

She tries not to giggle as she makes her way back to her First Ever. This is difficult in view of the three poker faces under the trio of hairdryers along the opposite wall.

Doesn't Mrs Willoughby know she's a dab hand with the scissors?

"Don't worry," the young man says. "We all have to start somewhere. I will too, one day. When I've finished studying Medicine."

"Medicine?" She gulps. Her First Ever is a man of distinction. She is privileged to be so near his head. She imagines trimming an opening through his locks into his great brain. "Are you going to be a doctor?"

Not just a doctor, he's going to be a surgeon. She should have guessed. She sees his and her reflections overlapping in the salon mirror and when she squints they are one.

His name is Edward. He asks her for a date. They cut a path into each other's worlds because they have this in common, their love of sharp instruments. Their love of tools to improve lives.

They get married, joining together like the paper figures she cut out as a child, only more perfectly sculpted, no hacked edges. She sees their two selves like two sides of a pair of scissors. Not one scissor – note – but a pair. They are that pair, forging through life, coming together in sleep. They get through bigger and bigger houses as he works longer and longer hours, chiselling his way up the surgeons' hierarchy, year upon year, while she styles wealthier and wealthier heads: film stars, actresses, top models, and when he flops in bed beside her after a twelve hour operation, she thinks only of the good he does: making incisions, cutting away tumours, sewing the skin together afterwards with the skill and precision befitting his profession. She understands why he is too tired to make babies.

But she becomes thirty-three and thirty-five and thirty-seven. Still no babies. He often doesn't come home at all any more. She sits in his study and rocks her fictional baby. Edward Junior should be cutting his teeth by now. She's cutting it fine if she wants babies, and yet they never speak about it – he is too busy and tired and never home. When she is next fertile, she will have to force sex on him, her legs scissored around him, and in a bittersweet voice say, "If you don't, Edward, I'll make you bleed like me." As she's thinking this, she rattles the drawers on top of his desk. Tiny drawers they are, like the drawers you get in haberdasheries, for cottons and needles and things. The second from top is locked. She takes the sharpest scissors from her sewing basket, the one that once belonged to Grandmother, and picks the lock. Beneath the shield of a Xeroxed medical article is a bundle of envelopes, looped together by an elastic band.

She snaps some of the envelopes from the rubber band, peers inside, and finds letters in an unfamiliar female hand. "He's got a bit on the side," she wails. "Like Father had." She shakes one of the envelopes and a photo falls out, of a child, a little girl with long hair, just like she had before she was shorn by the Barber. One letter, in particular, cuts her up. *My darling Ed, I hope you have recovered from your little operation "downstairs", my dear. I hope it will prove to be the least painful solution to our predicament. It is a devil for you having to keep Louisa secret, and for me having to lie to my husband about Louisa's true parentage, but in a few months time we will come out in the open as you suggest. When you leave Hilary, I will also tell my husband the truth about Louisa. We are in this together. It will work out, have no fear.*

He's got a child! The bastard has got a child!

He's had the Snip! The bastard has had the Snip!

She trembles as she hooks her fingers into the scissors and wedges the picture of the child between the blades. She cuts it into tiny triangles. The child has no hair. The child has no head. The child has been cut out of the picture.

She goes to the bathroom with the scissors. She sits on the edge of the bath, stroking the closed scissors up and down her arm, imagining it to be one of Edward's more sensitive bits, and asking herself, "Does he have any sensitive bits?" Then she levers the scissors open and doodles the sharpest point over her wrist where a tangle of veins throb blue. They look like messy threads. She imagines snipping through them and tying up the ends for a neat finish. Every time she thinks of Edward now, or the secret woman and child, she goes through this routine. Then one day, she makes a cut. The next day another. Then another, until she is cutting herself daily. It soothes her. It is all-encompassing for the duration of each bleed. Soon she needs to make bigger and bigger gashes until one day she unscrews the scissors from their joint pivot. Now she has only the one scissor. Detached, it is more like a scalpel. This is what it means to be separated: dangerous and uncontrollable. She makes a deep slash. When Edward finds out, he says she is unhinged. She is. From the other half. She lunges at the sofa with her scissor-scalpel, wondering if she'll find a baby inside. Maybe it's been hiding in there all this time, unnoticed. Sometimes she thinks she hears it scream, then realizes it's her own she can hear. It's not a sofa, after all. It's a hospital bed. They are cutting her hair, ready for later (and she thought she was the haircutter). They're shaving a patch. Later they will cut out a piece of her brain. It's called a lobotomy. Like they did to Jack Nicholson in *One Flew Over The Cuckoo's Nest*. One of those. Or is it a leucotomy? They are all the rage now. She's glad they're doing it. She likes the thought of them cutting into her head, especially if it'll change her brain. Edward will do it. He's the surgeon. He will make sure it's a success.

"We can offer you some sheltered work," the Occupational Therapy Lady says, visiting her in her sheltered flat.

Her husband has left her but the lady can offer her work. Her husband has left her, but that was years ago, before the mental hospital. She doesn't know why her husband left her, though it was probably to do with the thing they did to her brain. She's not been the same since, though the same as what? Several years have been cut out of her life and lost along the way, but it's OK to cut your losses; to sever all links with the past. Maybe that's what the mental hospital people taught her.

She pops the last grape in her mouth. There's a little bit of twig in her hand, a bit of vine, she supposes. She likes grapes. They remind her of hospitals and surgery.

"I want to cut hair," she tells the OT Lady.

"I don't think we're quite ready for that yet," says the OT Lady.

She doesn't argue the point. The OT suggests a painting class instead. She does as she's told, and paints vases of carnations or bowls of fruit every Monday evening. Her tutor suggests she gives her paintings more cutting edge. "Cutting edge," she thinks, trying to grasp a memory before it swims away, eel-like. "How about one of my Life Classes?" he suggests. She doesn't argue the point but slides a piece of charcoal across a scroll of paper while a twenty-year-old lounges in front of her, breasts like macaroons.

One day, the tutor asks her for a drink after the Monday night class. "Have you ever thought of modelling for the class?" he says over his pie and pint. She is slightly flattered. "You'd be a lovely person to draw. Lovely and round." He must mean fat. Like the women that Beryl Cook paints. There would be a catch, wouldn't there? Stupid to think there could be any sexual interest in her body; that she could possibly compete with the twenty-year-old macarooned waif who he kisses on the lips when she enters the pub. The girl looks like a

Louisa who will be loved and left by men like this. This is all conjecture and fancy, the place where edges blur.

She doesn't go back to the class. Maybe if she were to sharpen her body up, maybe if she had taut breasts instead of billowing great things, art tutors would desire her. She saves up her money, and on her mother's death, uses her inheritance to have a boob job and liposuction. They cut her open and suck out the blubber and put staples in her head while her mind enters a dream state…

It is an undertow, a habit, nothing more. There may be more shape to her body, but any pattern to her existence has come apart like a frayed dress. She used to know all about patterns, where to pin them on the fabric, though they were always flimsy; tearing at the touch of a nail. Unperturbed, she enters the blunt years, dabbling here and there with an inane air about her, wandering from class to class, job to job, year to year, hoping to sharpen her wits…

They're playing Pass the Parcel, like they did when she was a girl. Nurse Gail plonks on the piano for a few seconds and then stops. The parcel is with Marjorie. Look at the thing shaking around in her fingers, poor blighter. There are so many old dears here in fawn trousers with bottoms the size of cushions. She wonders what she's doing in a place full of septuagenarians and octogenarians. She's easily the youngest. Nearly all ladies too. Where are the men? "He cut me out of his will," she says to some pudding next to her, flossy head in her bosoms. "All he left me was his name." The music starts up again and stops when the parcel is in the Pudding's lap. She thinks, "How is the old pudding going to open the parcel with her rheumatoid fingers and vacant stare? Deary me." She reaches into the pocket of her cardigan for something she stuffed up her sleeve during this morning's arts and crafts session. They have rounded ends and are made for infant hands. They squeak. She takes the parcel from the Pudding's lap and starts snip-snipping. This is how you get into parcels. All he left her was his name. Mrs Edward Scissorhands. That's who she is. "Cutting it fine with these scissors of mine." There are pictures of kittens on the wrapping which she carries on cutting out, long after the parcel has resumed its journey. A few jagged, pawless kittens flutter from her lap. The Pudding's hair needs doing. She stands behind the Pudding, twists her hair up and clips it in place. Is it hair or faces that she cuts? It's faces, she decides, remembering the kittens, and she starts trying to cut round the Pudding's face, imagining the droopy skin and folds falling on the floor like paper.

SHARING SARAH

They shared Sarah like they shared everything else: the car, the flat, their shirts. Rick had her Mondays, Wednesdays and Fridays. Rob – Tuesdays, Thursdays and Sundays. Saturdays she did her own thing which suited them to a tee for they also shared an interest in football, but they kept a strict schedule as far as the rest of the week went. They also kept to tight boundaries: Rick having her top half. Anything below midway was strictly off-limits to Rick and he was happy keeping to his side of the bargain. He felt he was lucky being the one to have her bouncing breasts and sweet Martini lips. OK, so his side of the bargain didn't include her to-die-for legs, or her privates down there, but then he was falling short in the trouser region himself, so to speak, and didn't want her attention drawn to that matter. Luckily, she – for her part – also divided herself between Rick's top half and Rob's bottom half; their other halves being out-of-bounds to her as well.

The arrangement had come about after the best friends had got chatting to her in The Toad & Jug one Sunday night. They each fought for the lion's share of her attention and argued as to who should be the one to ask her out: Rob insisting it should be him as she'd served him first (she being the barmaid in said establishment), Rick equally insistent as she'd spent most of the time looking into his eyes, he maintained (75 per cent as opposed to 25 per cent.) They carried on their spat until Rick suggested they toss a coin and was on the verge of flipping it when Rob shook his head. "Let's put it to the young lady herself," he said. "We'll tell her that she's got two admirers – us two – and then see if she's got any preference." But Rick wanted to know how they would decide who should be the one to 'put it to the young lady'. And wouldn't that person have the unfair advantage? So they went back to Plan A and the coin-tossing: Rick doing the tossing, Rob the calling. Rob called Tails and Tails it was. So Rob swaggered over to the bar with his empty glass and cheesy chat-up line, Rick quick at his side to adjudicate. When Rob had said his piece, Sarah looked from one to the other – from Rick's well-formed face, to what she could see of Rob's raunchy hips.

"Now you should know better than forcing a girl to choose between two good pals," she said.

Rob, thinking himself to be the chosen one, assured Sarah that the other one could take it – they'd been friends since primary school, after all.

"Well, you both seem nice guys," she said. "What if I were to go out with you both to get to know you better? One tomorrow night, the other say Tuesday?"

"Us both?" The two men said in unison. Neither had entertained this as a possibility but, wishing to keep their options open, they agreed. Sarah left them to thrash it out between them as to who would get the first date. In a dim-lit corner of The Toad & Jug, the two men tossed a coin for the second time. This time, Rick called Heads and Heads it was, and so he asked her out on the Monday. (That being how Monday came to be one of his Days).

He took her out for a meal and the evening went well. He'd done well to be the one to take her out first. He'd done his best to create a good impression as first impressions counted for a lot, though at the back of his mind, as he chewed on his tuna steak, he knew it would be Rob's turn tomorrow. At the end of the evening he lent forward in the Fiesta he shared with Rob, hopeful of a kiss which might make her fall for him and thereby dispensing with the need for Rob. But she was already out of the car and thanking him for a wonderful evening, wiggling her fingers in a goodbye.

The following evening, when it was Rob's turn, Rick was on tenterhooks. He couldn't concentrate on any TV programme for thoughts of Sarah and Rob together, though Rob had promised No Funny Business on their first date. "Not even a kiss," Rick warned. "*We* didn't."

The two chums kept up their alternate dates with Sarah for the rest of the week and following Rob's third and strictly Platonic date on the Sunday, they were still none the wiser as to where Sarah's true affections lay. Rick was quite sure he had the edge over Rob until he heard the positive feedback from Rob's dates.

On the second Monday they decided Sarah should be phoned early evening to see if she had come to a decision. But they couldn't agree who should do the phoning since the person who had that task might be seen as putting pressure on her. On the other hand, the caller might sway Sarah into choosing him as he had taken the trouble to consider her feelings. Besides, they both agreed that the present arrangement was quite pleasant if you didn't think too much about what the other was getting up to. "What's yours is mine, Rick, anyway. Isn't that the way it's always worked with us?"

And so the routine and the division of the days with Sarah were established. That second Monday night, after a few drinks of Chablis at the Wine Bar, Rick got to kiss Sarah for the first time. He was sure now that he had made his claim on her. "A kiss changes everything," he told Rob when he got home. "So maybe you should just cancel your date for tomorrow." But Rob was having none of it. "One kiss doesn't a relationship make," he said, and the following evening, after a trip to the Multiplex, Rob was full of Sarah's thighs and boasting about how little of the film he'd seen. Rick felt all hot under the collar. "Did you kiss her?" he wanted to know. This for some reason was his overriding concern. Fortunately Rob shook his head. "She was pretending to watch the film, wasn't she?" Rick believed this to be true. When it came down to it, Rob was very much a Leg Man and got irritated when his lips were smeared in the same shade as a girl's, always wiping it off on the back of his sleeve after a heavy snog. Rick, on the other hand, loved to taste the fruity colours of a girl's lips, not minding a bit if his lips were stained plum or Hawaiian Nights. Fortunately for Rick, Sarah loved her lippy.

They thus carried on merrily enough with their – largely unspoken – arrangement for a few weeks, which seemed to give Sarah just as much of a buzz as it did the two of them. "Oh no you don't," she'd say, if hands crept too far up, or down as the case may be. It was she, in fact, who voiced the terms of the agreement. "Our territory is waist up, Rick," she'd say. "Rob's and mine is below. That way, none of us is being unfaithful if you think about it."

She'd put into words exactly how Rick was feeling. So Rob had slept with her, done it with her, but he hadn't had the pleasure of her lips and breasts. They were all his.

Rob, too, was happy enough with his lot, at first. He could go all the way, and he felt he'd landed in paradise when her legs wrapped round his shoulders and her honey-sweet vulva was ripe with longing.

But it was not long before Rob started to become dissatisfied with the arrangement and he thought perhaps that he'd drawn the short straw, after all. He thought about articulating his concerns and getting Rick to renegotiate the agreement which had never been formalized anyway, they'd all just drifted into it until the goalposts were hard to shift. Yet Rick seemed happy with his share, especially with his tackle being what it was (Rick had told Rob this in confidence one Saturday night not long ago, over a few bottles of Old Speckled Hen, and Rob had no reason to suspect things had changed). But what if Rick was lying? What if, in fact, he'd just said this to make Rob feel better and not in any danger, when really he and Sarah had been plotting together and were having the whole hog behind his back?

Rob decided to tackle Sarah about it one Thursday night at her flat. (Rob always saw her at her flat on Thursdays). "Sarah," he said, while stroking the flesh under her skirt between her stocking-tops and panties. "Has Rick – you know – ever tried it on with you?"

She suddenly crossed her legs, forcing his hand to retreat for the moment. "We've got an arrangement, Rob," she said. "And mine and Rick's is north of the equator!"

"But don't you ever feel tempted to go south?" he asked. "Curious?"

"Rick's impotent – I thought you knew – he just likes the intimacy of kisses and cuddles."

Rob was quiet for a moment, trying to decide on which thought to grasp from the multitude. "Well, it's all very well for him ... but it's much harder for me. It's so difficult making love without kissing, without feeling your boobs."

She uncrossed her legs. "You don't seem to have had much difficulty so far."

He held her shoulders. Shoulders were allowed. But he wanted her lips – lipstick or no. He felt like she was his whore, otherwise.

"If we kiss," he said. "Rick would be none the wiser. He need never know."

She seemed to entertain this for a moment with a furrowed brow and a screwed, protruding bottom lip.

"Wouldn't you like to kiss me, Sarah?"

"It would be deceitful. I couldn't cheat on Rick."

Rob sighed with frustration but he had to respect her fidelity. Then he had a thought. "But we've already broken the rules, Sarah," he said, reminding her about the oral sex. Their heads had enjoyed tails and therefore their heads might as well enjoy heads, mightn't they?

"I'll tell you what, Rob," she said. "I'll let you swap with Rick, but only if Rick agrees."

Rob thought this fair. It was like primary school when they did swapsies with cigarette cards or marbles when they got tired of them. He sung as he drove home. *Lips like strawberry wine*. For that's how he imagined Sarah's lips would taste. He couldn't get them out of his mind. First thing in the morning, last thing at night, and threading through his dreams. He was quite prepared to forego all the sex, just for this one pleasure.

When he got home, he burst into the flat, rubbing his hands together. "Sarah and I would like to swap, Rick," he said. "It's my turn for heads, and yours for tails. That's fair, isn't it?"

But the look on Rick's purpling face was one of horror. "No! I won't swap," he said. "What use is tails to me in my bleedin' condition?"

"Ah, but Sarah could cure all that with her magical touch." Rob caressed the air with an expressive hand. "You know what they say – use it or lose it."

"No. I'm quite happy as I am, thank you." And with that Rick got up and walked out of the room which was a sure sign to Rob that the subject was closed and not up for negotiation.

The matter wasn't referred to again that evening, and Rick went on his Friday date as usual with Sarah, though things were preying on his mind and he wasn't able to enjoy their kissing as he usually did. When it came to

Rob's next date on the Sunday – Rick reaffirmed his side of the bargain. "I wanna keep heads, Rob, pal. OK?"

But now Rick could no longer relax when Rob was out with Sarah. He hoped he could trust Rob – he thought he could – but the very fact that Rob had *wanted* to swap was enough to unsteady things. Now whenever it was one of Rob's nights with Sarah, Rick brooded about the flat, channel-hopping, not properly engaged with the TV programmes as he fiddled with the sellotaped-up TV remote in his hand, wondering, dreading. Whenever he heard the key in the door on Rob's return he tried to look composed, but there was this mistrustful silence, this avoidance of the subject of Sarah. And when it came to his own nights out with Sarah, there was now also an avoidance of the subject of Rob.

Things were getting so strained between the former best friends that when the next Saturday came, Rick didn't bother accompanying Rob to The Jack Of Spades which they usually frequented ahead of Match of The Day, anticipating the big matches and how much footage their team would get. Instead, Rick sat drinking and brooding on his bed, the street lamp casting a dreary orange glow on his hunched-forward figure. Presently, he pawed out some smutty mags from under his bed, trying to work himself up in the seedy light but brewer's droop had already set in. He wouldn't swap. He wouldn't give up heads. Heads was his. He punched his right fist into his left resolutely.

Then he came to a decision. He would broach the subject when Rob returned from The Jack Of Spades. He wouldn't let it fester any longer. In fact, wasn't that Rob now – turning into their street, collar up against the biting air? Rick decided to go down there himself. He would face Rob head on, man to man – somehow it was easier out of doors than in the suffocating atmosphere of the flat where taboos thickened like the dust in the corners.

"Rob, it's about Sarah..."

"Has something happened?"

"No, nothing like that ... can we take a walk round the block?

"Make it quick then – our match might be on first."

Rick opened his mouth to speak but first a police car came blasting past in a car chase up a one-way street and then they witnessed a fight between two skimpily dressed teenaged girls – the smaller one, taking off her high-heeled shoe and clubbing the other girl with its spiked end. It was Saturday night, after all. Finally they crossed the car park behind The Toad & Jug where one car in particular caught their eye. The car was bouncing and moving slightly, of its own volition. It didn't take the two men long to work out that there was someone in the car. Two people in fact. One with her legs sticking up in an ungainly way against the rear seat window while a great hulk of a man humped away. Rob peered through one window, Rick the other. "Sarah!" they both exclaimed in unison, but she was too busy having the mother of all snogs once the humping had ceased.

Rob rapped on the window. "Hey, put him down, Sarah!"

Rick hammered on the other window. "What about our arrangement?"

Sarah put herself back into her top and heaved herself up, opening the window slightly. "Hi boys," she said. "I'd like you to meet Mike."

"Never mind Mike!" Rick was furious. "What about us? You're cheating on us both!"

"No, I've not cheated. I just discovered a loophole in our agreement. And a very tasty loophole at that," she said, riffling Mike's hair.

"What loophole?"

"It's Saturday," she said. "And no one said anything about Saturdays."

This was indeed true. Neither of them had been prepared to give up their football night for Sarah.

And so now Sarah is shared three ways – Mike getting the added bonus of heads and tails as compensation for only having her Saturdays. The introduction of a third person has helped to dispel the intensity of Rick's paranoia, while Rob has never raised the subject of heads again.

ON REACHING YOUR HALF CENTURY

There comes a day when you realize you're never going to be great at anything. For many of your haven't-yet-made-it contemporaries it was around the age of forty-two or three, while you battled on in hope, against all the odds. "Life begins at forty," you said, defiantly, ten years ago, even though there were bright twenty-somethings breathing down your neck and even brighter thirty-somethings passing you on their ever-upward climb while you and your friends rationalized your situation with talk of "late blossomings". When the odd flower bloomed on your metaphorical cherry tree at the age of forty-five, you knew you and your friends had to be right as you looked forward to a whole orchard. When the orchard didn't happen and you knocked on the door of fifty – fifty! you! who've always been fifteen at heart – you and your friends (fewer by now: one or two having died prematurely, the odd one having become unbearably successful) talked of "fifty being the new forty".

Now you've already reached that formidable milestone. Outside your house there's just one remaining balloon where forty-eight hours ago there were several – taut, jolly, blue – bobbing in the sun. "To vintage 19– " you said at your birthday do, clinking glasses with your chums, but once the party had dissipated, that illusion of greatness and achievement that you've long assumed would be yours one day – it was just a matter of time – burst like one of your blue balloons at the feet of your unsung little life. You don't think it'll happen now, not in this lifetime anyway (for you are at an age where future lifetimes have taken on new meaning.) Oh you're good at what you do. Very good even. No-one could argue with that. You've been in the *Gazette* several times these past few years and once you were mentioned in the *Independent*, though your name was misspelt and a few years had somehow got lost off your age so it would have been easy for more distant friends to have missed your fifteen minutes entirely, but no matter. You have a crinkled copy of the article, sepia and torn by now, mouldering in a drawer somewhere. You even received an award once, from the local arts council, and when you received it you thought, Damien Hirst move aside (or whoever was the biggest hot shot in the art world at the time – you can't remember now).

So yes, you're good at what you do. Very good. But greatness needs the head start of youth, you now realize. You did start young. You could always be counted on to have a crayon or a piece of chalk in your hand. But maybe if someone had spotted your singing ability instead and you'd got onto 'Opportunity Knocks' you'd now be a household brand. The fact that the peak of your singing phase amounted to a few rounds of 'Old Harry The Lavatory Cleaner' on the annual school coach trip to Brecon Beacons is by the by. With a bit of encouragement and nurturing in the right measure, you're convinced that Old Harry could have been out of the privy and destined for bigger things. The same could be said of any number of your childhood talents. "Has an aptitude for mimicry" Miss Dawson wrote in your second year school report. The fact that you mimicked illness after illness to get out of athletics, which you loathed with a vengeance because you were usually last in everything, was neither here nor there. You say 'usually' because there was that brief spell when you had that growth spurt and could suddenly get your legs over the hurdles without knocking them down; you could suddenly wheel the shot round and round instead of the shot spinning you round and round before take off. If someone had called you aside at that crucial time to put in the extra training you could have been an athlete of Olympic proportions by now.

Then there was the way you could fold your ear into a little parcel for a few seconds without it popping out – you could do it with both ears, though your right ear was your stronger one – and your school friends crowded round your desk to watch. It was then that you had a fleeting glimpse of yourself in the circus, people queuing up and paying to see your clever trick.

When you look back you could weep at the thought of these and other undeveloped talents having gone to seed, but you reached an age– about fifteen or sixteen – where you had to think about careers. Various occupations had been suggested to you since the age of twelve: including teacher, civil servant, advertizing, the army (the latter as a result of your having expressed a desire for foreign travel after a school trip skiing in Austria). But you postponed all that by going to art college for two years where you built up a good portfolio and got signs that this was the path you were meant to be taking. You inherited an easel and spent your days creating small masterpieces, courtesy of the DHSS (as it was known then) and your father's wages. You figured that being single-minded and dedicated was the way to greatness, rather than "keeping your options open" or having "several fingers in many pies" which smacked to you of "Jack of all trades, master of none" until your parents told you it was high time you got off your backside and earned your keep. You thought it a good idea too, excited at the prospect of your own dosh to spend on clothes and records and discos instead of cadging off your old man. It was for this reason you didn't care about the details of your job (a little pen-pushing number, taxing only a fraction of your academic skills and nothing of your creative ability). It was all new to you, this working business: the lunchtime booze-ups, the office parties, the legendary Friday nights – the novelty not wearing off for a couple of years.

When it did, you started applying for other posts. Cinema Manager Trainee. You thought you'd apply for that one because you were quite a film buff on the quiet, weren't you? You were offered it but you turned it down anyway, because the interviewer had mentioned in passing the potential detrimental effects on your social life, and how did you feel about that? You smiled and told him it didn't bother you one jot but on reflection it did. If only you'd taken that job when you were offered it you could have your own chain of cinemas by now. Then there was that idea you and your friend had about opening an exotic pet shop. Your friend had a couple of iguanas and a python and knew a thing or two about their housing needs and feeding habits and mating rituals. But the python died and your friend joined the Hong Kong police and so you never soared to David Attenborough heights. You can't remember if that was just before or just after your brief sojourn into playwriting. An agent, described as the best on both sides of the Atlantic, asked you for lunch in London one time, but then you broke your leg and had to postpone it, and by the time your leg was out of plaster and you were free to travel, the particular agent in question had moved on to pastures new. But you were young enough to know there'd be plenty of other boats: a whole flotilla in the guise of all those other options you dabbled with: dog-breeding, astrology, farrier. (Farrier? Really? You? Who doesn't know one end of a horse from another?) You sigh, thinking of the things we nearly do, the lives we nearly lead, the people we nearly marry. You can't help but conclude that there's a whole character we nearly are!

But you narrowed down your options long ago. You trained to be a Social Worker, and this – plus your relationship (at least until your divorce nine years ago) and your eventual family – ate up the years. In fact, you didn't even have time to watch as the years spilled out and ran away from you. You couldn't catch them any more or gather them up like you used to. Your calling in life took a back seat and to call it such was perhaps elevating it to a status it never really achieved. At best, you dabbled. You put your own greatness on hold while trying to foster it in your offspring: (maybe it was they who would make their indelible mark on the world instead, you thought, with a mixture of pride and envy). You remembered the head start of youth theory again and promised yourself that your children would want for nothing as you Lived to Work (even though this was anathema to you in your youth). You'd read about Type A personalities and saw that the words rigid, obsessive, driven and heart attack could now apply to you as you hit a crisis in your career. You clashed with your line manager and were passed over for promotion, the politics of it all getting in the way of what you had always thought of – perhaps naïvely – as people-type work, until you were signed off with stress. This was a sign you thought, a sign for you to hear your Calling and get back to your easel. You decided to leave the rat race and trusted yourself to the universe (as well as the good sense of your GP who helped secure your long-term Sickness Benefit). It seemed you had made the right choice when the arts council award and your piece in the *Independent* materialized, followed by one or two moderately successful exhibitions. But it was spasmodic and largely local: you weren't about to get your Big Break and the financial and practical problems put a strain on your family life, resulting in its eventual breakdown.

Now you had nothing or no-one to constrain you as you threw yourself into your creations. You kept hearing that the market was getting tougher and tougher; that more and more people were doing what you were doing; that fewer and fewer people were buying; that today everything was conceptual – but it didn't deter you. You went on believing in yourself (somebody had to), year in, year out, and your friends all had stories of the starving artist in his garret who eventual makes it while you tried to ignore the loudening voice at the back of your brain which cried: Fifty Beckons! People have made it by fifty! People are Prime Minister by fifty, sometimes into their second term!

You tried to hang onto the fact that you honed this path for yourself, though you're slowly realizing now that it may perhaps be the wrong path. You'd like to go back to the crossroads but you get the distinct feeling that if you did you'd find them overgrown. No worries: you've reached your half century and it's taken you this long but you'll settle for less than great, knowing that when you're old and greyer you'll never have to be a has-been.

50 today, the balloon says. Two days ago it was part of a triplet: fat and bonny in the sun. Now there's just a shrivelled singleton waving about on the gatepost in the pouring rain, like a stranded whale at sea. You clutch hold of it, squashing it in the palm of your hand, too deflated to burst. Then you smile with resignation at your lot in life.

BOO

"Look, it's BOO! It is! Kids, ask grandpa! Oh BOO, still with that beatific look."

That's when I hit the coastal wall at 60 mph, wiping the smile clean off my face.

Looking back though, it was a godsend, seeing them out of the blue after thirty odd years, and in such an unexpected part of the country. You could say they saved my life.

You see, my owners were going to trade me in for a new one: it's a feeling you get in your chassis. I got wind of it a few weeks before, that day they took me out to Plymouth. (They got wind of it too, you could say.)

"We want the A3121 to Ugborough," Mr Dunroamin said, stopping in a layby and pawing the map in Mrs Dunroamin's charge. "It's more direct for the southern part of Plymouth."

My heart had just started pumping again, ready to show just how fleet of wheel I still could be if you treat me right, with a bit of respect and TLC, when the old flatulence problem returned, didn't it? Pop pop, all through Yealmpton and Brixton, I could have died. It's a nerve thing you get. Spot of the old anxiety, especially with those two, watching my every move. Perhaps if they'd been less rough with my backside, slamming it down three or four times over the sore and smelly objects that filled my bowel: lethal umbrellas, that old picnic table and chairs, some horse manure for Mr Dunroamin's father, then I might have been able to control myself better. Course, they were none too pleased.

"Listen to that God awful noise," Mr Dunroamin groaned. "I'd say the rust bucket has had its day."

Rust bucket? Me? If there's such a thing as poetic

justice, then it happened a bit later on that journey when they couldn't find signs to the Hoe. "Toilets," Mr Dunroamin demanded. "If we don't find loos soon, I'll mess my pants." At that I started pop-popping again, couldn't help myself.

That's when Mrs Dunroamin said, "You're right, darling. On its last wheels, I'd say," and not a hint of regret in her voice, though I whinnied when they started moving me off again. Thinking, I won't go quietly.

It was different when I first went to live with them over twenty years ago. They still lived in Essex, back then, and took good care of me. They washed me and took me out daily, showing me off to all their friends. They'd take me up new motorway sections to different parts of the country I'd never seen before until one day they changed jobs and moved across to the South West. That was a bit of a wrench because I was born in Essex (1969) and spent my formative years there with a big tumbly kind of family and their licky dog who loved me to bits for seven long happy years. But times and financial situations change. My next guardian was a young student who delighted in the fact that I was starting to go to seed. He looked after me in a neglectful sort of way, making sure I got my daily rough-and-tumble during my rebellious years. Stickers on my forehead, knee deep in mud, you know the sort of thing. We saw life, me and my student. Then he graduated and decided I belonged with the past, so he got a mate of his to perform a bit of surgery on my bodywork; that's when the Dunroamins snapped me up, though it was Mrs D who fell in love me with me first, caressing me a treat, and so began their roamin years.

But wear and tear gradually take their toll and the Dunroamins bought many other models over the years to take them from A to B, while still hanging on to me for

Old Time's Sake or for a quick nostalgic romp, pretending they were still in their twenties. Like that Wednesday afternoon a few weeks ago, which they'd both taken off work. Through their open kitchen door I heard Mrs D say to Mr D, all sort of frisky as you do, "What about the garage, honeypops? Bet that'll do the trick."

They scuttled inside, shuffling into my lap. (I was still good for something then.) "Take me for a ride in our old passion wagon," she said, writhing into my gearstick which I was none too happy about.

He was bouncing about on top of her, causing pains in my groin, when suddenly he said, "It's no good, darling. I can't."

(Thank God, I thought. Glad that someone else's gearstick was in worse nick than mine.)

She sat up then, buttoning up her blouse and looking at herself in that small rectangular place that forms part of my internal landscape: the place where I do most of my reflecting.

"Is it me? Do you want to trade me in for a younger model?"

"Course not, darling," he said. "My bits aren't in such GWO as they used to be, that's all."

Ah, a reprieve, I thought. So vintage can conquer over youthful perfection.

But they wouldn't go away, those feelings you get in your chassis. Especially when you're stuck in one black room day after day, only stale air in your lungs. You start remembering the good times when they took you up the M1 to Yorkshire or across the M4 to Wales, or curling around A roads in the remotes of Scotland, the invigorating air spinning through your vents.

Mr Dunroamin should have understood. The doctor told him he needed more exercise and fresh air; that he was on course for coronary troubles if he didn't make lifestyle changes. Mrs Dunroamin should have understood: she's one of those who hates being cooped all day in the office, hates too much dark – every winter you hear her complaining of Seasonal Affective Disorder.

It was all right for them. Good-as-New and The-Body-Beautiful were becoming important concepts in the minds of the Dunroamins. I knew it was only a matter of time. They'd get themselves a younger model with a sleek figure, a newborn probably, who wouldn't gobble up the juice, who wouldn't fart or embarrass them on the way to Plymouth, who'd move their life into a lower gear, smoothly, quietly, resting discreetly while they puffed and panted in the gym, doing their dumbbels.

It wasn't so much the thought of being traded in, as whether I'd get another home at my time of life, or whether I'd end my days on the scrap heap, my only worth in my internal organs, giving life to another after my demise.

It was a normal day like any other. Mr Dunroamin sloshed a bucket of soapy water in one of my eyes where weeks of grit and grime had lodged from the occasional muddy outing. Needless to say, most of the suds slopped ineffectually down my chin, and poor vision looked set to continue.

I felt my bones creaking a bit as Mr Dunroamin climbed in, trying to make himself as comfortable as possible as he put on his driving glasses. Then he said to Mrs Dunroamin as she wriggled in my lap beside him, "I thought we'd take a trip to that secondhand car dealer's today. You know, that one on the other side of Paignton."

Told you. Feelings in my chassis. I had to suppress my choke while Mr Dunroamin started the old heart up. It usually beats like a dream, my old ticker, but it felt all sort of heavy that day.

"Don't like the sound of that," Mr Dunroamin said.

"Can you hear that murmur?"

He touched my gearstick but it wasn't hitting the spot. "Bloody thing," he cursed. "Always getting stuck."

"Here, let me drive," Mrs D said, and I felt the source of my prowess grinding into begrudged action, though she didn't have the magic touch any more either.

"Definitely time it went," he said. "Agreed?"

"Agreed. We've had some good times in this thing but I'm past sentimentalism. Give me comfort any day."

We started moving. Let me tell you, my feet didn't touch the ground. They may not be the fastest runners in the world, but they're solid, they've got a good tread on them, make no mistake. Mr Dunroamin let some air into my lungs as we jogged through a rather industrial bit en route to Paignton. Before long we came to a standstill behind rows of red eyes, staring through me indifferently. My younger brothers and sisters, and they thought I was past-it too; that I couldn't compare with their smooth unbruised skin; that I shouldn't really be out at my time of life without a major facelift. I knew as well that I could further embarrass the Dunroamins with a one-man protest, refusing to budge, breaking down (breaking wind even), or having a right old tantrum in the queue. But I'd have been playing into their hands, so I moved off, gritting my teeth as the ozone whistled through them for half a mile.

That's when I heard my name being called.

"Look, it's BOO! It is. BOO, still with that beatific look! Kids, ask grandpa! Tell them, grandpa!"

Hearing my name like that, my name of old, and her voice, well, it took me back to the flat coast of the east with its pebbles and fishermen's huts. Took me back to the windmills of Kent where they used to take me out with their dog, the happy tumbly family singing there were ten in the bed and the little one said roll over, roll over; where there was always someone spending the night with me, layering me with blankets, and the sweet warm breath of children and dog. And here she was, one of those happy tumbly children with happy tumbly children of her own.

What with hearing them say BOO again, and my eyes all misty with sea spray and homesickness, well, it caused me to spin off course, didn't it? Smack bang into the sea wall.

My mouth took the brunt of the prang. So did Mr Dunroamin's, swelling up nicely like the buckling in my own, while Mrs Dunroamin had a beaut of a bruise over her right eye to match the crack in mine. Apart from that, they walked away without a scar, the Dunroamins. Without a backward glance.

As for me, the Happy Tumblies reclaimed me. They restored me and took me back to my roots where you can catch me, some Sundays, hanging out with all the old crowd, comparing our name tags, SOO and LOO and POO, seeing who's in the best nick.

I'm pleased to say that big solid bodies with fancy curves can still turn heads in the right places. So if you see me, all you sixties veterans, don't forget to smile and hoot your horn, and if you're really lucky you'll see me smile back, because they don't make smiles like this any more.

FAMILY TRADITION

The smack was passed down from mother to daughter (there having been a paucity of sons for generations) and the smack started with Elsie. At least, that was as far back as Tanya could trace it if she took the direct line up to the higher branches of the tree. Things tended to get a bit sketchy pre-Elsie who passed the smack down through Pearl to Pattie and eventually to Tanya, like a genetic defect.

Tanya now walked up Arbroath Street holding her daughter's hand tight. "This road tips like a seesaw," Jodie said as they hiked up from The Blacksmiths' Arms through the dusting of snow. Beyond the top end of the seesaw you could see the remains of the dark satanic mill where Elsie had worked as a child.

"Look at my footprints, mummy." Jodie delighted at their imprints in the thin and frozen snow.

Tanya squeezed out a smile, though she could hear the words of her mother in her head: That's not snow. That's just a smattering.

Tanya's mother had spoken of whole winters during her childhood when she'd opened the front door onto a thick plate of ice, spanning all the way down the steep hill to the factory in Kilmarnock Street where she had started work at fifteen. Tanya felt like a Poncey Southerner (a term of her father's), as she and Jodie tried to get to grips with the icy surface and slope. An elderly woman overtook them, tramping up the hill at a steady pace with four bags of shopping. She was clearly one of the old school. Out in it first thing, battling the elements.

Winters in Pearl's and Elsie's day were even harsher still, no doubt: frozen rivers to skate on, swirling blizzards, huge drifts of snow as depicted in Christmas cards, without the cosiness. Tanya wondered even whether the smack arose from the harshness of the weather and conditions, in which case environmental factors might be of possible significance in its aetiology and its maintenance.

When Elsie was married she and her husband continued to live in Arbroath Street, where Elsie passed on the smack to daughter Pearl. A great, calloused hand walloping her like a bat was how Tanya's grandmother described it, earned for the smallest of misdemeanours. Pearl used to say it almost with affection, and more than a little pride, for it was a great family tradition. The batted hand around the backs of her legs had honed her into shape and better ways, she maintained; had stopped her chucking her pa's shoes in the tub or putting her muddy footprints all over her ma's newly-scrubbed floor.

Maybe Pearl was still saying such things. Tanya had yet to find out, having not seen some of her family for fifteen years. In fact – since leaving home at the age of sixteen. She now lived far away from them, in the Poncey South. Her mother and father had visited the Poncey South only the once, six years ago, when Jodie was born. Tanya had thought it her duty to tell them of their granddaughter. But she was coming here now to try and put a perspective on things, now that she was a mother of a school-age child herself.

Tanya paused outside Number 22. "Your great great grandmother Elsie lived in that house as a child, Jodie," she said. Then she pointed across at Number 19. "And your great grandmother Pearl lived here when she was first married."

"You said my great granny lives with my granny at Number 51."

"She does." Tanya feared she was overwhelming

Jodie with too much family history, though her reasons for coming up here were partly for Jodie's sake too. Jodie had expressed a curiosity about them, and a desire to meet them. At first, Tanya had made excuses: (it's too far, it's too expensive, granny and I don't always see eye to eye), until she questioned her motives for keeping Jodie from the senior women.

But as she paused for breath opposite Number 19, where Pearl had lived for much of her married life, Tanya had second and third thoughts about the trip up here. She thought about Pearl who had passed on the smack to Pattie. Many more photos of Pearl's younger years had survived than Elsie's. Those pictures were to Tanya like something straight out of a kitchen-sink drama. She remembered a typical one of Pearl, as a young mother, standing in her pinny in the doorway of Number 19, her hair spraying out of its clips like a trailing plant. She had two daughters at her feet, one on her hip. The child sitting on the step with her arms folded and her socks falling down was Pattie. Something about that picture used to get to Tanya. Something about her mother's sulky expression, a budding recalcitrance maybe, for she would have already been initiated into the smack. She would have already felt it across her bare buttocks for being a bad child. For beating down the neighbours' daffodils with a stick. For saying 'oh God' or 'Jesus Christ' which was taking the Lord's name in vain (though if it was prefixed by 'good' as in 'Good Lord' or 'Good God' then she sometimes escaped a spanking for some reason). Her mother was full of such stories, having long since internalized the smack's significance in child-rearing. Like Pearl before her, Pattie's attitude was that you had to honour it and treat it with respect when it was passed down to you, since it was part of the family tradition. At least, this was Pattie's stance as an adult, though Tanya suspected the girl with the baggy socks might have viewed it differently. Sometimes Tanya had glimpsed cracks in her mother's defence. "Because it was done to me, that's why!" she'd shouted, her eyes flashing like hazard-warning lights. Sometimes Tanya thought she'd witnessed an internal struggle at the centre of her mother, though her mother always defended her actions. It was easier that way, Tanya supposed.

Tanya didn't know much about genetics, but her limited knowledge told her that defects were supposed to become weaker with each subsequent generation, not stronger.

Her attention now turned to Jodie who was counting the house numbers as they huffed and puffed to the top of the seesaw street. "Forty-seven, forty-nine, fifty-one! Mummy, fifty-one!"

*

Inside Number 51, Pearl's face was set in a frown of disapproval. Pearl only had three settings: sour, very sour and ultra sour. At the moment it was set on Very. Tanya thought this as her father took photographs of the assembled gathering. It was all coming back, the smells, the nuances, the bossiness of her mother, the weakness of her father. But she was doing it for Jodie, though she had her own mission, too, which she hoped to accomplish the following day.

Once night time had fallen, Tanya tucked Jodie into the divan where she herself had slept as a child. "Night night," she said, kissing Jodie on the forehead. She was about to shut the curtains but Jodie was all excited about some lights she could see through the window, beyond the glittering roofs. "A drum with lights," was how Jodie described it. Tanya laughed for the first time since she had set foot back in the house. "It's the gas works, Jodie." Jodie looked at her as if to say, So what? What's so funny? To Jodie it was a beautiful ring of lights through a new window full of secrets. Tanya was glad that Jodie could find beauty in the stark scenery of the industrial north. But as she stepped out of the bedroom Jodie started protesting. "Where are you going, mummy? Mummy?" At home, Jodie frequently slept in Tanya's bed. "Shh now. Be a big girl and go to sleep." Tanya felt all ears on her as she backed onto the landing. "I'll leave the curtains open so you can look out at the drum of lights."

Tanya could imagine Pearl nudging Pattie. *Fancy indulging the child like that.*

She lay awake half the night in the third bedroom, next-door to her mother and father. She could hear Pearl snoring in the downstairs bedroom directly below hers, the old mattress creaking every so often. The mattress belonged to that same generation of furniture as the old green armchair in the front room, which Pearl spent the most part of the day in. Tanya pictured a child in a pretty frock sitting in that armchair. The armchair swamped her. The child's mother was furiously spraying funnels of starch over her father's shirt collar. Off camera, there was a little girl in a pretty dress being smacked to bits. For what, Tanya didn't know. When the child got up from the chair she was older. Fourteen. Sixteen, even. She had her arms folded in defiance of her mother. The girl and her mother shouted at each other across the ironing board, both red-faced, their eyes like fried eggs, more whites than yolks. Then the girl's face was being pounded by the slap for her insolence, her rebellious adolescence. The girl's head was swimming like a fish bowl, the fish inside drunk, their bubbles clashing. "I'm leaving this fucking hole," the girl screamed at last, slamming the door behind her.

The girl left home for good the next day and fended

for herself. She lived without the smack until the men came giving her good money for it. They wanted her to pass on the smack – very specific they were too as to where exactly they wanted it. Sometimes they wanted to pass on their smack and she tucked the money up her garter and all she felt was the disembodied smack smack smack until she got caught out with Jodie.

*

When Tanya surfaced the following morning, Pearl was already in the green armchair by the window as if she'd never left it to take some sleep. Tanya lifted a net curtain to gauge the weather, just as Jodie clattered into the front room shivering; her sleeves covering her hands. "I'm cold, mummy."

"Cold?" Pearl puffed. "You don't know you're born, child," she said, on her Sour Setting. Tanya could just about remember when there was ice on the inside of the windows. She could remember the pretty patterns it left and her mother scraping it off with the blade of a table knife. The windows no longer rattled as Tanya peered out.

"Is there still some snow, mummy?"

"A bit."

Tanya could see a few tenacious clumps of grey ice, here and there, in the north-facing front gardens, especially up this end where the higher gradient made it cooler.

Pearl sighed and turned her setting up to Very. "Pwf. They don't make snow like they used to."

Tanya's mother switched on the radio after breakfast and sang along to the oldies as she washed up. Tanya's father hadn't gone to work yet. He was on the twilight shift at the factory all this week. In between the songs, they discussed the smack on the radio. The smack was going to be made illegal if it made a mark on the body.

Tanya turned the radio up so they could all hear. None of them were listening except her father who said the same thing had been done in Scotland with the over threes. He nudged Tanya while Pattie quizzed her granddaughter about her school Down South. "I know this joke," he said. "Jock says to Mack, 'what'll ya be giving y'wee laddie for his fourth birthday then, Mack?' and Mack says 'a smack.' 'Och aye,' says Jock, 'it becomes legal then, doesnae it?'" Tanya looked away from her father's poor attempt at a joke and his even poorer apology for a Scottish accent which was about as far away from Scotland as Arbroath Street was to Arbroath. But really it was the women's attention she wanted, though they'd have probably laughed aloud at the report and some of the comments being made on the radio phone-in. There was a wisp of silence when Pattie and Pearl might have just caught the tail-end of what sounded to Tanya like an enlightened discussion had not Jodie piped up with, "Are we going out, mummy? Mummy? MUMMY!"

Tanya frowned at her daughter, annoyed that she'd cut across talk of the important piece of legislation which proposed to outlaw the smack. It was a lost opportunity and Tanya snapped at Jodie.

She then remembered her reason for coming up here in the first place, and checked herself. She turned to Jodie. "Yes, we are going out." She said it in a softer tone than previously. "There's still plenty of snow up on the high ground – we'll take a walk up there, shall we?"

"Oh cool!"

Tanya went to the cupboard under the stairs where the old red wellingtons she'd worn as a child were still stowed. They smelt a bit musty, but once she'd cleaned off the cobwebs she saw they'd do perfectly for Jodie. "Here, Jodie. You'll need these."

"I don't want to wear them," Jodie said, more as a

whine than anything, before gradually building it up to a full-blown tantrum. "No! I want to wear my shoes!" she screeched repeatedly, no matter what Tanya said about their inadequacy. Tanya could feel herself under scrutiny by the senior women as she tried to squash Jodie's mule-kicking right foot into one of the wellingtons. She could hear the tuts from Pearl behind her back, her face surely on Ultra Sour by now. Pattie, too, was watching the unfolding episode with incredulity, hands on hips. Tanya knew what they were both thinking. They were expecting her to pass on the family tradition.

Tanya fled into the hall. God knows she'd nearly kept up the family tradition. Jodie was no angel. She'd had her phases: trying it on, those horrid screams she used to do when she didn't want to do something, the way she used to smack out at Tanya, like the gene had skipped a generation. Then, Tanya could have easily passed it on to her daughter, with knobs on. But she'd gritted her teeth, she didn't want to leave a legacy, so she sublimated the smack. She belted the wall or she passed it on to the men who still paid her occasionally.

Tanya returned to the front room with new resolve. "No wellies, no walk in the snow, Jodie. It's as simple as that."

She sensed more head-shaking from both her mother and grandmother but felt a glimmer of triumph as Jodie's chary right foot hovered above one of the red wellingtons. Tanya went to her aid, holding the sides of each wellington firm while Jodie pushed down with one foot, then the other.

Outside, Tanya and Jodie climbed to the top of Arbroath Street before crossing Black Moors Lane where the snow was treacherous and smeared with mud. It was on a dark winter's morning, fifteen years ago, when Tanya had last stood at the bus stop in Black Moors Lane, staring at the yellow, street-lit pavements full of slush. She waited there, coat buttoned up, duffel bag on her shoulder, stomping up and down, trying to keep out the biting wind. She had watched every approaching vehicle, blowing on her hands, thinking every passing red lorry was her bus, cursing when it wasn't. Then the bus came and took her into town. Light streaks started appearing in the sky by the time she got to town, and from there she took a train to the Poncey South. Mission accomplished.

Now she had another mission to fulfil. She took hold of Jodie's gloved hand as they climbed the steps, cobbled with iced footprints. They trudged on upwards, past the viaduct, taking the short cut through the lacy covering of snow. Great spikes of grass were sticking up through the snow, though by the time they got to the highest point, with the mill on their left and the cemetery to their right, the holes in the snow had all but disappeared.

Jodie was curious about the old mill – now a working museum – but Tanya said they could go another day. Besides, Jodie soon forgot the mill once she saw the thickness of the snow inside the cemetery. So far so good, Tanya thought. It was going to plan, and though she knew that some might find it morbid bringing a young child up here, she also knew that to Jodie the cemetery was just a place with a lot of crosses where dead people rested. Jodie skipped through the gate and seemed oblivious to the bleakness of the wind up here, though Tanya felt it whipping at her extremities. Earth stood hard as iron, she sung to herself. Whoever wrote that carol must have had this place in mind, she thought.

They criss-crossed through the crosses and headstones, leaving footprints several inches deep, until Tanya stopped by a tilting headstone, wiping the snow away from the engraved letters with her glove. "This is the one," she said. "Can you read what it says, Jodie?"

"It says – Elsa!"
"Clever girl. And Elsie was your– "
"Great great grandmother!"
"That's right. She used to work at the mill."

Tanya had a fleeting vision of Elsie's dim skin beneath the Saturn Rings Sunday hat. The rest of the week Elsie would have been in her mill gear. Tanya fancied she remembered a crumpled photo of her great grandmother in a head shawl, held together by toughened hands. She could almost feel those batted hands vibrating down the generations. But it ends here, she thought as she crouched down and scooped out a hole in the snow over Elsie's plot. At the bottom of the hole she buried the smack. Buried it as deep as the worms. Then she covered it over and patted the mound. She'd returned the smack from whence it came and when the snow melted the smack would melt with it.

"What are you doing, mummy? Have you planted something?"

Still crouching, Tanya swivelled round and tucked Jodie's fawn hair into her hood. "Yes," she said. "I planted a kiss." She placed one on Jodie's forehead. "Like this."

She hoped Jodie would pass it on.

Then she brushed the crystals of ice from her gloves and stood up, Jodie scampering on ahead in the red wellingtons that had caused so much furore. Now they were a source of delight as Jodie jumped on icy puddles near the mill. Mother and daughter slithered on downwards, eventually returning to the lacy snow through which great swathes of green were emerging.

They crunched back down the steps, crossed Black Moors Lane and stood at the top of Arbroath Street. They looked to the bottom of the road where the sun was out already. It shone on the pavement and started creeping up the hill.

AN ANGEL AT MY DOOR

Dorothy Duff has a new neighbour at last. A woman. She wondered who she'd be getting on her right, and she's glad there are no children. It's always awfully sad to see children, or worse, little babies moving into the neighbourhood. There are a few in the vicinity, it has to be said, though they tend to be housed all together. Jerry to her left is young enough – he's middle-aged – and provides enough youthful zeal to these otherwise elderly parts. Nevertheless she's looking forward to a good old chinwag with someone more her own age.

The new lady is called Mary, and when Mary's family have settled her in and waved goodbye, Dorothy wastes no time in introductions, giving her new neighbour a rundown of all the area's inhabitants.

"Ah, you'll soon settle in here, Mary. It gets a bit blowy up here sometimes but it's pleasant, especially now all the daffs are coming up."

It's always difficult, moving to a new area – especially if it's to be your last – so Dorothy tries to help Mary feel at home.

"So what sort of door are you getting then, Mary?" (Home improvements are always a good ice-breaker.)

"Door?"

"Well – I call 'em doors," she says, thinking about her own ten-year-old pink granite one. Jerry on her left has a slate one. "My wife wanted something understated," Jerry told her, almost apologetically, when Dorothy first moved in next to him, as though he would have chosen something grander. "Oh it's very nice, Jerry," she lied. Sometimes she worries about coming across as too flirtatious with Jerry, in case her husband should pop in for an impromptu visit, with a nice bunch of carnations, or something seasonal, which he does from time to time. But of course her husband married again, didn't he, when death did them part, so she considers it reasonable to have a laugh and a joke and a flirt with Jerry. He is young enough to be her son, or her toy boy, but all the elderly ladies make a fuss of him and mother him, as they do with some of the other forty and fifty-something men over the way. Jerry takes it all in his stride. He used to have some do-gooding job in the voluntary sector so he's used to dealing with people from all walks of death.

But after a few weeks, Dorothy still knows very little about her new neighbour, Mary. "I came here for a bit of peace and quiet, Dorothy," is how their conversations usually end (never mind the fact that Mary has a stream of visitors).

Or even worse: "Do you mind, Dorothy? I've got a busy day ahead. I worked hard in the theatre for years and if I'd known it was going to be this noisy I'd have taken the 'other option' and had done with it."

"Oh well, excuse me for breathing," says Dorothy. Today Mary's getting her new door put in, replacing the temporary wooden one. This must be the busy day ahead to which her neighbour was referring. When the job's done, and the professionals have finished digging and installing and straightening, Dorothy decides to put her differences with Mary aside for the time being and swoons over her choice of door: an opulent white marble affair.

"Oh very poash, Mary, I'm sure."

"No, not posh, Dorothy. Just tasteful."

"Oh yes," Dorothy agrees. "Just like mine."

Perhaps she only imagined she heard Mary say, no, I said tasteful. Mary wouldn't have said that, a well-bred lady like that, especially as they are neighbours. But Mary seems to grow in popularity with every passing week, with all manner of people planting all manner of bright flowers in her garden, removing any shrivelled petals and watering the beds, lending her patch a luxuriant look. It reminds Dorothy of where she used to live; where it was important to keep up with your neighbours, for they soon gossiped, herself included, if standards started slipping

She looks on wistfully at the withered offerings outside her own door and feels both ashamed and competitive. When her husband next pays her a visit, he at once observes the ostentatious display of flowers next-door and apologizes for the paltry primroses, already starting to wilt in their pot. It wasn't always thus: they used to keep a neat lawn at their other place, and jolly flowers in window boxes under their flouncy nets. Her husband clears his throat. He has some devastating news. He and his present wife are moving hundreds of miles away to Scotland to be near his wife's children and grandchildren. "I know you'll understand, Dorothy. I know I have your blessing and that my happiness is what you would want."

The deserter!

Dorothy wishes she and her husband had adopted children when she knew she couldn't have any. Children would be loyal and come and visit their dear departed mum. Now she faces a bleak future without visitors, while all and sundry – children and grandchildren, people from Mary's High Church, and all those luvvies from the theatre – crowd the next-door property, many of them not even pensive or weepy like most visitors to these parts.

"What about *my* peace and quiet?" says one very disgruntled Dorothy after a particularly hectic day next-door. "All your visitors are blocking my view and trespassing on my borders."

"Nonsense," says Mary. "My visitors are always mindful. They don't go trampling where they shouldn't."

Dorothy falls into a peeved silence. Mary is a classy lady, no-one can dispute that, but it's hard keeping up with all her airs and graces and fancy trappings, and resentment starts to creep in. She turns to Jerry on her left. "Oh she's dead poash, her on my other side. Thinks she's a cut above with all those flowers and all that marble. Talk about fancy."

Jerry smiles and tries to keep the peace. At least she's got one decent neighbour. He's a nice chap, Jerry; she should stick with him. She decides not to speak to Mary. That'll serve her right. Then she'll have no one to turn to. Just the plain earth and grass to her right. But far from feeling spurned, Mary seems to delight in her new-found quiet and when she requires company, just carries on a conversation with Jerry straight over Dorothy. She talks about the cultivation of flowers and was that your wife and children came to see you today, Jerry? Very charming, too.

Don't mind me, Dorothy fumes to herself. But her beef isn't with Jerry. Poor bloke has just got dragged into Mary's snare. "D'you mind?" she says to Mary, one day. "Jerry's *my* neighbour. We got on swimmingly before you came along."

"Well, poor old Jerry is all I can say. Do you think he wants to be next to your sniping and bickering and petty ways, morning, noon and night?"

"Oh and do you think he wants the pong of half of Kew Gardens wafting over to him while he's trying to sleep? He's got an allergy to anything with pink foliage."

"Now then, ladies," Jerry says, fearing the development of a neighbourhood dispute. As a former chairperson of a Residents' Association he's got his work cut out here, mediating between the stiffs. But Dorothy doesn't want mediation. Perhaps she doesn't like Mary all that much, after all. She wishes it was empty again next-door and if she could move to another property she honestly would. In any case, Jerry doesn't see it as much of a dispute at all. Not like when those two old boys squabbled over the way – those brothers who'd fought all their life long, over women, property, work, inheritance, and they were damned if they were going to put a sock in it just because they were six feet under. The noise of their wrangling was fit to near wake the dead, whereas their deathly silences were another matter. Whispers went round the neighbourhood, and Jerry was called in to do his bit, and now bygones are bygones where the brothers are concerned.

But whenever Dorothy complains to Jerry about those get-togethers next-door – "and let's face it, Jerry, she's no spring chicken either", he merely says, "Oh I like a bit of life" or "a bit of jollity doesn't disturb me", though Dorothy finds it very disrespectful to the neighbourhood as a whole. But with Jerry not really onside, she suffers in silence, wearing a stiff upper lip, until one morning an angel appears.

Gobsmacked, she stares at the spanking new structure on the adjacent land. She turns to Jerry. "She may have been High Church, but did she get planning permission to put up that flipping angel?"

"Probably from God Almighty," says Jerry.

Then a voice on her other side says, "I thought you said Gob Almighty. That would be an apt description of our neighbour, wouldn't it?"

Dorothy wheels round at this nasty remark, which she could have sworn issued from Mary's lips, but to her horror finds Mary fast asleep. Besides, the accusatory voice sounded less like Mary's. It must have been the angel's then – it was a female voice without a doubt.

Dorothy is quiet all day, lest the angel should come out with more aspersions. It's at night, when all her neighbours are asleep, that her senses are sharper and she lies awake waiting for the angel to cast another judgement. She gazes up at its marble wings, glowing with moonlight. Angels aren't usually malevolent – are they? – though she can't see the expression on the face of this one. Dorothy wonders if it wasn't some trick of Mary's – something she learned in the theatre; a sort of ventriloquism.

Being a garrulous sort of soul, Dorothy can't keep quiet for long and tries to engage Mary in conversation the next day, and the next. "There's no need to take a huff with me," she says.

On the third day, Dorothy hears the voice again. *Dotty No Mates. Dotty No Mates.*

"Oh, how childish," she says, again barking at Mary until Jerry puts her straight. "Oh you won't get an answer from Mary," he says. "Didn't you know? She's taken a vow of silence."

Dorothy shakes her head, perplexed. She can't be doing with silence, though she did wish for it. She tries engaging Jerry but he's resumed conversation with the old boy on his left. In her own enforced silence, Dorothy feels lonely. Her husband has left for Scotland, Mary is on retreat, and Jerry is preferring the company on his other side. She whispers to the angel at night. I was a good Christian in my day, I was really, and I may not have been High Church but I said my prayers, and put my Sunday best on for Christenings and weddings, and tried not to drift off in the vicar's sermons. And I know it's wrong to covert, especially in such a hallowed neighbourhood, but my husband always kept a tidy lawn and we always had cheery flowers to put in our window and a statue on the patio.

She looks up at her neglected plot and borders with deep sorrow. She always looked down on such people but she must be lowering the tone of the neighbourhood with her unkempt grass and ugly clods of earth, her slushy leaves and molehills, not to mention her grubby door – once her pride and joy. No wonder Jerry prefers the view on his other side! No wonder Mary has gone on retreat!

Before long, she starts to welcome Mary's visitors who call by regularly, in spite of Mary's silence. One or two of them, in particular, begin straying over the boundaries and stop to take in the neighbouring houses. One of them starts tidying up the detritus building up at Dorothy's door. "There, that's better," she says. "It's looking less neglected now." The next time she comes the visitor plants a few flowers and waters Dorothy's lawn with TLC

That night, Dorothy has a long, satisfying sleep. She dreams of a proper chimney on her roof. She can feel it being placed in prime position, and on waking finds an angel of her own, watching over her with a beatific smile.

She hears the voice again. "Oh hark at you, with your new angel."

It may be Mary's voice, it may be her own. It may be next-door's angel.

But Dorothy doesn't care. She's keeping up with the Joneses again, and death is no excuse for not doing so.

GOD ONLINE

They wanted to interview me, earlier, on TV, about my new prototype of human being. I declined, of course. Dr Starbuck is much better at dealing with the media than I. The good doctor and his research team have been working at the Institute *of Human Biotechnology in California* for three decades on my new model which is in the final stages of development. They've ironed out many of the flaws from the old model and if successful the new model will replace the old within generations.

No, I prefer dealing with online queries. I have a site – God's New Prototype. My trademark logo: rays of light and my celestial hands fashioning my creation. My fingers are androgynous, one hand pale, the other dark. There's a discussion in the forum at the moment, where I'm putting in a rare appearance. (My appearance is no biggie, these days).

InnerTiger: (ginger cat avatar, front paws aloft on scratching post): God, I've just watched the programme 'Model Citizens' with your spokesman talking about your new prototype. But I'm happy with the current one, thank you very much. I just don't know why you allow yourself to be pressured by the scientists. In our day, you were mysterious. That was part of your attraction. We've always accepted our 'design faults', as Dr Starbuck calls them, as coming with the territory, though I prefer the term imperfections.

UrbanArtiste4: (black and white arty avi of girl on bar stool in chic bar): So agree, IT. Love the avi btw.

ScouseBrenda: (avi with two plump women smiling):

Good God, I'm hanging on to my old body. Warts and all. No one's tampering with my body. I thought we were meant to be imperfect anyway. My fella's old man always did reckon, God, that you were just some scientist and we were your guinea pigs.

Me: I can understand your concerns, but the new model will by no means be perfect, just a distinct improvement on the current one. In terms of waste disposal, for instance, the liquids and solids sites of the present model were constructed too close together, causing contamination, malfunction, all sorts of problems. In the new model we can see a much better layout of sites. Of course, future generations will ideally be designed without the need for waste disposal at all but at the moment that's still in the planning stages.

Sammie_Robinson: (b & w avi of small boy in long shorts and 1960s haircut): Son of a gun! You gotta tell these scientist guys, Dawkins and the rest, they can't dictate to you. You're God for Chrissake. Stand up to the sons of a b, pardon my language.

InnerTiger: With respect, Almighty God, you're starting to sound just like Dr Starbuck and the rest. Waste disposal! Why go fiddling about with nature anyway? OK, bodily fluids are a bit messy, but they've stood the test of time, haven't they?

UrbanArtiste4: :D

ScouseBrenda: Waste disposal, my arse! Sorry God, but I like a good dump I do. Call me crude, and I know I shouldn't say this in your holy presence but there's nothing beats a good ole crap. OK, it's a bit messy, and there's all that bog roll and all those loos to clean and all those sewers but there's jobs to be had in wee and crap, make no mistake.

UrbanArtiste4: ROFL

Me: I take your point, Sammie. But I have to adopt the language of scientists these days to get my point across. You have heard about the competition from the Silicon Giants and the Robot manufacturers and the Artificial Intelligence people. I have to stay in the market.

@InnerTiger, we're not just talking waste disposal. The new model also contains many risk reduction features. The prototype has a finely tuned limbic system, and those areas of the brain concerned with the higher mental processes have been enhanced at the expense of what can now be regarded as 'primitive brain' which, though it served your predecessors well, is less appropriate for the advanced species we have today. The neurotransmitter concerned with self-harm, for instance, has been isolated and modified. This particular neurotransmitter, thought to be associated with many forms of destructive behaviour, will mean a lot more co-operative type behaviour in future, as well as a reduction in conflict, aggression, war and so on.

InnerTiger: That is to be applauded, God, don't get me wrong. The eradication of war is a good thing for the future of mankind. No one could argue with that but we all need a bit of conflict in life. For growth. For spiritual development, as you know. Conflict has its place, God, surely. I'm not called Inner Tiger for nothing!

ScouseBrenda: @ IT. Sooo true. Folks have been

fighting for all time. You can get some clever dicks in some poncey American place working for God, twiddling about with brains and that, but people don't change that much. No more wars, that'll be the day. We all want that but I can't imagine no more little spats with him indoors, no kiss and make up. Our lives ud be a dull load of nothing without em. Thats part of relationships, part of life. *You* put the kettle on, no *you* I dunnit last time. All that. I think God's losing the plot. I think he's lost control, I do.

Me: Inner Tiger and Scouse Brenda, there'll still be conflict. Rest assured. Dr Starbuck's research team aren't yet at the stage of eliminating it completely and, as you say, wouldn't wish to.

LouLittleton: (Bible avi): Your a fake! Youll burn in hell 4 messing with the lords creations. Wanting to do away with the way women has their babies, this is all predicted in revelation

InnerTiger: Yes, what is all this about doing away with reproduction? Many women are angry & feel cheated by it.

ScouseBrenda: What, no babies? Is that what your saying? No babies? Jesus Christ!

Me: I've watched and listened to and observed women down the centuries and the general consensus is that women are dissatisfied with the whole shebang – the pain and so forth, not to mention the fluid loss every month for something they may only need two or three times in their lives. It's a very wasteful design in terms of days lost through malfunction. In the latest study of Dr

Starbuck's, 24% of women have expressed a wish to do away with reproduction altogether. This rises to a staggering 68% if we could come up with an alternative. One of the current model's main reasons for reproducing itself is its inbuilt tendency to deteriorate over time, resulting in its eradication. This has been the bane of this model since its creation. Today we expect a lot more from our bodies and in a couple of generations we could have a model that spontaneously regenerates, which would indeed eliminate the need for reproduction.

UrbanArtiste4: Hey, I could go for that ☺

InnerTiger: Call me cynical, God, but it sounds like a Capitalist plot. You know, too much wastage in pregnancy and childbirth and child-rearing. Much more economical to have everlasting man – or woman. Especially woman. I just feel that you're not in control any more, God. The scientists are the one with the power, the ones funded by the omnipotent governments. The people's God – you – the one we know and love and grew up with, you're just an honorary nowadays. A patron, a sleeping partner, though partner makes it sound like you're an equal which you're not. OK, so it was your design to start with, you still take the credit, but others are cashing in. It's as if you're God in name only; that you've had to give in to popular and scientific pressure.

Sammie_Robinson: Couldn't have said it better myself, Inner Tiger. This guy has had his balls ripped off by the bad guys, dammit.

Me: Quite the opposite. I oversee the research team and I'm not planning on early retirement quite yet – I just prefer to delegate. It was a lot of responsibility in the old days, too many chiefs, and not enough Indians. Only the one chief, in fact, and all the flak on my shoulders. No, that's an enormous weight, for any person, even God! I like to see myself as a flexible god, moving with the times, and the times are very democratic, thank god. ☺

InnerTiger: With respect, God Almighty, a lot of us have had enough and that's why the numbers for SOB are growing daily. You know, Save Our Bodies. It's time to stand up, God, and be counted. I don't want to go on forever. I want to die and have a normal burial like my parents and grandparents and all my ancestors. And I want the same for my children and my children's children if, yourself willing, they're still able to have children. But when it comes to the day of reckoning, God, will you be able to account for your actions? Will you be able to face the cold reality of everlasting bodies and souls who wanted out? Who've made you redundant? It's not too late, God. There's plenty of us still rooting for you. We love you. We would die for you so you can live!

Sammie_Robinson: Yay!

ScouseBrenda: SOB? I wanna join that!

InnerTiger: @ Brenda. Message me and I can see if there's an SOB branch in your area. If not, how about starting one? They do all sorts of things – talks in schools, rallies, there was a small one in Hyde Park a few months ago, but numbers are growing, I believe. They campaign to preserve that mystery and omnipotence of God. We don't want God demystified. Keep God Sacred – for God's sake!

Me: Your fears are very typical and have been noted,

my friends, but I hope I've managed to allay some of them at least. People are bound to be sceptical at first, and sad to see the old model being phased out, but our new design will be a great success, of that I'm certain.

This will run and run, but I've gone offline now. In fact, I crashed the debate at this point. Well, I could see all those angry trolls and dyed-in-the-wool fundamentalists, queuing up, hardly able to spell for the red venom in their eyes and heads as they pounded their digits on keyboards, spitting fire that my site kept freezing on them. It helps to be God, at times like this.

Besides, when I see that, I know that the model upgrade is a must ☺.

TO THE WIRE

1. The Life

Sammy McRed kicked off 3.01 pm one autumn afternoon and his father had great plans for him as he did all his sons. "Practise your talents every day, son," he said, priming Sammy for a leading role in life because there are many rival clans in this world, but none so great as the McBlues.

Sammy's first fifteen years were full of hope as he learned to become a team player at home, and away from home.

By the time Sammy was seventeen, his family started expecting things from him. They wanted him to have a goal in life. He wanted one too, and one day when he saw one of the McBlue girls swaggering about between a pair of trees on the edge of the McBlues' estate, Sammy rushed in ahead of his brothers. It wasn't often he saw a girl from such an inviting angle and she had such an open, smiling mouth. Like she was saying, "Come on, Sammy. I'm all yours." He made his way steadily towards her, for to win a McBlue girl would be a prize indeed. He came at her, arms outstretched, but in his eagerness went flying into the nearby tree instead. *Oh, he's hit the woodwork!*

But Sammy had been taught not to dwell on his mistakes and kept on pursuing the McBlue girl. She was called Nettie, and Nettie was becoming a goal in life. Well, getting his leg over with her. "But let me warn you, Sammy," she said to him one day. "If any of my family catch you making a play for me, they'll fight you tooth and nail." Well, Sammy had never been one to duck a challenge. So he got round some of the weaker McBlues so he could practise his passion as Nettie lay on the grass, her legs open and inviting. "I'm nearly there, Nettie," he said to her one day with an impressive thrust of his left ball.

"You're nowhere near, Sammy."

"Just wide," he thought.

But Sammy felt the pressure from his father to win Nettie and break down those four die-hard defenders of the McBlue family name. But with his father on his case all the time, Sammy spent the next few years kicking about with his brothers, flirting with women, hitting the bars – a bit of travel up and down the country. He was having a ball. There was plenty of time to settle down, though it wasn't going down well with his father who clutched his head in his hands when he heard that David McBlue had swept one of Sammy's cousins off her feet and married her. (1-0). Sammy's father was apoplectic, bellowing at Sammy's brothers (especially those whose role it was to protect the McRed girls.) Then he had a go at Sammy. *You're pushing thirty, Sammy. It's time you settled down. So come on, look sharp.*

The pressure was on. Sammy thought about his next strategy while his brothers spent the next few years successfully coming between David McBlue and his new wife, breaking up their relationship to prevent a baby. Meanwhile Sammy concentrated on getting himself a job with potential. It was in a small firm where many of the McBlues worked – (for not all the McBlues put up a big resistance) – and Sammy got a foot in the door.

Over the next few years, the company expanded and Sammy fought to become head of his section, employing more McReds, so that in the firm as a whole, one side broke away from the usual patterns of working, Sammy's side, while the other defended the McBlue ethos. Each side was happy arguing its corner, until Sammy started attacking the McBlue ways. "We've got to move forward all the time," he told the McReds. Sammy saw it as his mission, his goal in life, and God knows he'd tried the best part of forty years searching for one. Of course, he was on McBlue ground, but bit by bit they were succumbing to the onslaught of change. Sammy and the McReds continued pressing forward until the McBlue way of doing things had almost receded, but the last remaining McBlue, seeing he was under attack, said to Sammy, "I wouldn't get on the wrong side of me. I'm the last bastion, and I'll defend this firm to the end."

Sammy battled on regardless, ignoring the McBlue, thinking he'd achieved a goal in life at last. Then he saw the arbitrator had the flag up for offside, and his goal was disallowed.

The arbitrator then checked his calendar and let out three short whistles. It was time to review the first half of Sammy's life and that of his brothers.

Sammy's father wasn't happy with the McRed performance thus far and gave all his sons a good dressing-down, especially Sammy. "You've just spent the first forty-five years pissing about!"

Sammy knew he'd have to do better in the next half of his life. He returned to life a new man having decided his next goal should be a wife.

But on his forty-seventh birthday, Sammy got caught up in a bit of bother when he saw his cousin, Gail, being pursued by some of the McBlue brothers outside the local nightclub. Gail's bodyguard, Gilly McRed, had taken a tumble and Gail stood there, mouth open and defenceless.

Sammy wasn't used to being the protective sort, but Gail was in distress and Sammy's brothers weren't doing their job so he rushed over to help her, only to find he was being impeded by three of the McBlue bruisers.

"You looking for a fight, ugly?" Big Mick McBlue said. "I fancy her, so mind your own." Other muscly McBlues shot in from nowhere. Sammy looked behind for his own brothers but they were being overpowered by the McBlues. Big Mick turned towards Gail. "You're all mine, darling," he said, ready to make a move on her. "Stay away, Sammy, you're making matters worse," Gail shouted, but Sammy was having none of it. He tussled and tackled Big Mick, then he thought he'd use his head. He swung it back, all ready to head-butt Big Mick but Big Mick ducked so that Sammy clocked poor Gail instead. She screamed and fell. "Now look what you've gone and done, Sammy!" she shouted, as Big Mick played the hero and rescued her in his arms, leaving a hapless Sammy looking on, horrified gasps and cheers of "own goal!" ringing in his ears.

Sammy knew he'd let the side down and the McBlues were already cheering. *Two nil two nil two nil, two nil two nil, too – hoo ni – hil.* Sammy was threatening to lose his rag as they entered the nightclub. He kept jostling Big Mick, but luckily he didn't see red. He saw yellow which was a warning before the red. He had to make sure he didn't see red though, otherwise the bouncer would chuck him out so he heeded the warning of the yellow and decided to play the midfield.

Sammy got work in Europe and his father looked hopeful of a goal. None of the McBlues had ever got work in Europe (though anyone who was anyone went to Europe), and Sammy sent home letters from Barcelona and Madrid and Milan, describing his achievements, and his father jumped up and down. "A goal! At long last, a goal!" (2-1). But the celebrations were soon curtailed. Sammy and the boys needed more goals if they were to succeed in life. A wife. A child. Children. They were still trailing in the game of life and none of the other

McRed boys looked likely to produce any additions to their clan. *Come on, Sammy. You still have thirty years left on the clock!*

So Sammy came home to concentrate on this one aim.

The opportunity soon presented itself when Sammy met Mae-Wynne. Mae-Wynne liked to play a dangerous game that appealed to Sammy's adventurous nature. He started to wine and dine Mae-Wynne, leading to a few passionate displays; he thought he'd met his match until one day he saw her looking very intimate with Rico McBlue. "Win her back," Sammy's father screamed. "Fucking fight for her." Sammy did, using all the tactics he'd learned over the years, but Mae-Wynne went backwards and forwards between her two rivals, playing one against the other. Both Sammy and Rico fought to make her his. *The only way to secure her, Sammy, is to marry her!* So Sammy took her out one evening, dancing with her in perfect rhythm and building up to popping the question, when along came Rico, showing his body off to her, moving around her as if he were God. But she was just as evasive with Rico, she seemed to elude them both, until one day Sammy saw her out with a baby. He wasted no time in approaching her. "It's my baby, isn't it, Mae-Wynne? I'm the daddy." She had that guarded look in her eye. "Might be, might not. Might be Rico's." Sammy thought for a while. "It doesn't matter who's the blood father," he said, thinking of the foreign imports adopted into the McRed family. "It's who'll make the best father, and I'll prove to you I'm the one." Sammy was soon impressing Mae-Wynne with his demonstrations of fatherhood: offering to take care of the baby whenever he could, and generally getting to know the child. But Sammy's father was impatient. "Don't fucking play at it, Sammy. Get custody of the kid."

Then one day, when Sammy was strolling the pram

through the park beside Mae-Wynne, he heard footsteps thundering behind him. "That baby is mine!" Rico panted, but Sammy confronted Rico. "I've been like a father, and I'm on my way to making the child mine." With that, he started pushing the pram away but Rico didn't like it one bit, he pulled at Sammy until he fell flat on his face, then snatched the child in full view of Mae-Wynne, as well as the gathering McReds and McBlues who each wanted the child for their own, and not to mention the growing crowd in the park who cheered one side and booed the other. "Penalty!" the McRed faithful yelled, while a policeman blew his whistle and went after Rico, ensuring the child was handed back to the mother. "I hardly touched him," Rico said, but the policeman could see that Sammy was injured, and charged Rico with aggressive abduction.

When it went to court, the defence for the McBlues maintained that Rico had only been trying to win back the child for the McBlues, but the defence was too weak beside Sammy's powerful argument, his dedication, his sheer determination, and the judge ruled that the child should carry the name of McRed. The McRed supporters jumped up and down in the public gallery. "A goal! Another goal!"

Now it was honours even (2-2) as Sammy moved towards the autumn of his life. But the McBlues had a new doggedness about them. Old Johnny McBlue, who'd spent most of his life sitting around on a bench, got off his backside and decided to study for a degree. Not that the McReds believed for one moment that Old Johnny would see it through – he was said to drink a lot, his brain cells were slowing down, and he wasn't seen as a serious threat. Sometimes they'd see him working in a corner of his field, writing notes, and wondered what his game was. The McReds were in for a big shock when Old Johnny surprised them all with first-class honours. Now the McBlues were ahead again in the game of life. (3-2).

By the time Sammy was in his eighties, a number of his brothers were exhausted with the hurly-burly of life and their father decided to retire two of them. Sammy needed help to win the game of life from another source. Alan McRed, the brother who joined Sammy in close partnership for the final years, was full of ideas. "It's not too late to get ourselves another goal, Sammy, and draw level with the McBlues. An absorbing hobby. That's what we'll aim for. But we have to work together, Sammy. That's what's been lacking. A bit of team work."

Sammy's brother kept coming up with ideas. "What about cycling, Sammy? I'll provide the bike and you can do the pedalling." Sammy still had a good left leg on him, though his right was letting him down a bit these days; it just didn't seem to have the same power on the pedal, sometimes missing it altogether. *You must keep active right up until the very end, son.* So Sammy persevered with the cycling, he worked hard, but he knew it'd never amount to a hobby. "What about writing then?" his brother suggested. "I'll provide the ideas and you come up with the script, the final punchline, OK? The McBlues have never been published." Sammy did his best, and though he was on a hat-trick, he was very tired and his thoughts kept going off at tangents. "Tell you what, Sammy," his brother said. "You come up with the ideas and leave the finished product to me." Sammy found this was a better role for him, and together he and Alan McRed found the perfect partnership. The McBlues, having got wind of the book, tried to write one of their own but it was the McRed book that was snapped up by publishers, blasting into the bestseller's list in no time at all. *We've drawn level!* (3-3). The McReds were ecstatic. The success of the book had given them all a point in life, though Sammy was ninety years old now and just playing out time. Then he heard a voice say, "we're giving you another three years to live." Three years! It wasn't long. It was now or never, and it gave him a desperate focus, like he'd moved onto another plane. A spiritual plane. The McBlues peppered him with taunts, *going down going down going down, going down going down too – hoo he – ell,* but Sammy was hell-bent on proving them wrong. He read lots, always in pursuit of the meaning of life, springing about the place with a hungry purpose. And then eureka! "God! I've found God!" he cheered, half way through his ninety-second year, and the McReds were jubilant because he seemed to have given them more than a point in life. "Another goal!" they cried. "Right in the dying seconds!" (4-3).

And then God looked at His watch at 4.51 pm on that final day and gave three short blasts of His final whistle.

2. Post-Life Analysis

- Good evening. People have been talking about it for ages. Would the McBlues see red? Would the McReds have the blues? I've got Dougal Stewart with me in the studio tonight. Dougal, let's take a look at their lives in a bit more detail – here we see that wasted opportunity in Sammy's eighteenth year. He should have made something of that, shouldn't he?

- He should have, Tony. There were two wasted chances in his teens. First he hit the woodwork when trying to seduce Nettie and then here – I'm telling you, it wasn't a pretty ball when he was trying to make love to her! (Laughs).

- Oh a real poor-looking ball, Dougal. (Laughs too).
- He fluffs it completely, Tony! (Laughs again).

- But when David McBlue married the McRed girl, that really put the pressure on the McReds, didn't it?

- Aye, Tony. The McReds were sleeping and the McBlue wedding was fully deserved. Watch the way he whisks her off her feet. Oh that's a sweet bride.

- But that wedding got the McReds to refocus and gradually break up the newly-weds – the last thing they need here is a McBlue child.

- Aye, all credit to the McReds – they had a job to do and they did it.

- Here's Sammy again, full of renewed resolve after his mid-life evaluation, then he sees his cousin in danger outside the nightclub, and goes over to protect her.

- But what was he doing up there, Tony? There should have been three or four of his brothers protecting her – that's their job, especially with her bodyguard down – but instead Sammy does his best to deflect Big Mick from making a play for Gail, and what does he do? Head-butts her instead.

- Such a shame – he's driven her right into the arms of Big Mick, hasn't he?

- Dead right, Tony. Big Mick comes up smelling of roses. He's a hero now in Gail's books. But in all fairness it was Sammy's brothers at fault.

- Absolutely. It's still bothering Sammy though, isn't it? Here we see him having a tussle with Big Mick just inside the club and nearly gets thrown out.

- Aye, that was stupid, Tony, right under the bouncer's nose an' all. He was lucky to get away with just a warning.

- Frustration, wasn't it? But then he gets his life back on track over the next ten, fifteen years, and he does really well here, getting work in Europe. His goal in life here isn't dramatic but the culmination of steady progress.

- Aye, but Dad's still not happy, is he? He knows the McBlues have still achieved more in life – especially with women. Sammy's thinking, "I'm sixty, I'm two thirds through my life, I better get myself a wife and wee child." Here we see him meet a lovely woman, Mae-Wynne, tries to keep hold of her, but look at this from Rico McBlue, he's so sharp here, and Mae-Wynne is nearly swept off her feet. Watch how he curls his arm around her body. Beautiful move.

- But none of them can get her, Dougal, can they? Most of the time she's moving backwards and forwards between Sammy and Rico.

- Aye, Tony, but then along comes the baby and Sammy's really cute here, look at the way he handles the baby, a real natural, but then Rico challenges him and snatches the child, here we have it again, oh absolutely no doubt about it, he tugged Sammy, then tripped him up. The policeman had no choice but to charge him.

- Yeah, it was spot on, Dougal. And Sammy works his magic in court, really puts his foot down and wins the right to be the child's father.

- Aye, this is a poor spell for the McBlues.

- Until Old Johnny comes off his bench and takes them all by surprise.

- Aye, Old Johnny can be deceptive, Tony. He's given a set piece of work to do, beavers away quietly, and comes up first class!

- Absolutely. The McReds need some fresh ideas now, and Alan McRed does well here, he comes up with ideas for a hobby, the cycling and so on, though Sammy can't keep his foot on the pedal, can he?

- He's just having a bad foot day, isn't he? (Laughs).

- You had some of those in your time, didn't you, Dougal?

- Aye, we've all had a few of those, Tony.

- Sammy's just very tired by now. Watch him here – and here again – his brother tosses ideas across to him but he does nothing with them.

- Aye, he is tired, and his brother takes a leading role in the book and delivers the finished product. Look at the way it's written, the passion, the timing – a real peach.

- And suddenly it's game on, Dougal.

- Aye, though Sammy's just happy running down the clock now. (Laughs). He's ninety, Tony. He'll settle for a point in life.

- But when Sammy knows he's only got three years left on this earth – he wants one last go. Look at him here. A man with a mission.

- Aye, just look at the spring in his step. Absolutely breathtaking for a man in his final year. He's hungry for something more, sees a path opening up, and then bingo – he finds God! Magnificent.

- Went right to the wire, didn't it?

- It did. Where is this place anyway?

- What the wire? I don't know, Dougal, but people keep going there. (Laughs)

- Must be good then, Tony. (Laughs too).

- So all in all, a good win for the McReds, Dougal?

- Aye, but take nothing away from the McBlues. They did really well.

- Indeed. Thanks, Dougal. Well, that's all we've got time for. Hope you enjoyed it at home and we'll be back for coverage of more premiere lives at the same time next week. Goodnight.

BIG MOTHER

Left Ear walks into the Diary Room, and makes itself comfortable in the Big Mother chair.

"Hello, Left Ear," comes the disembodied voice from the other side of the wall.

"Hello Big Mother."

"Left Ear, can you give me your first nomination, please?

"My first nomination is Right Ear."

There's a pregnant pause from the other side.

"Can you give me your reason, Left Ear?"

"Yes." Left Ear fiddles with its lobe. "Oh this is really difficult. All the Body Parts are so nice but Right Ear never hears properly. It doesn't listen. We're supposed to be working as a pair, right?"

Another pause from Big Mother.

"Can you elaborate on that?"

"Yes, the other night, I was trying to listen to Heart, you know, the non-physical part of Heart, but Right Ear was just listening to the boom-boom boom-boom, so it blocked out the sound with a plug which I thought was a bit unnecessary. A bit rude, in fact. I just think one ear can do the job of two – and that other Body Parts are of more use to the Big Mother body as a whole.

"Can I have your second nomination now, please?"

"My second nomination is going to have to be Mouth. I don't always have a good relationship with Mouth. Sometimes it's too loud and the noise reverberates. I just think it's more dispensable than other Body Parts. Hands and Eyes are just as good communicators as well as having other skills to offer."

"Thank you, Left Ear. Can you just confirm for me your two nominations?"

"Yes. Right Ear and Mouth."

"Thank you, Left Ear."

"Thanks, Big Mother."

Left Ear rises from the seat and leaves the Diary Room.

Left Ear rejoins Right Ear on the sofa, just as Left Eye is called to the Diary Room (the order they are called being in alphabetical order). Left Ear is feeling lousy, wondering if it's burning round the edges with guilt. Still, Right Ear may well do the same to Left Ear when its turn comes. There's no good worrying about it – it's the name of the game. Left Ear looks across at Mouth which is smiling away, oblivious. Left Ear wonders which Body Part will be left in the final reckoning. Arms and Legs are looking confident at the moment but Left Ear has a good idea who should win. Body Parts aren't allowed to discuss their personal nominations, though some seem to find this more difficult than others. Mouth nearly blabbed before Hair was voted out last week, and Left Foot nearly put its foot in it, predictably. Both Hands were also finding it hard not to signal to other Body Parts.

Two hours after Nominations, Left Ear is just trying to switch off to the Breasts which can't stop stressing how much spice they add to the Big Mother Body, when a row starts.

It's Right Hand, contorted into a fist. "You better watch your back, Back."

Back didn't see Right Hand coming (only the Eyes did, though Left Ear swears it heard something brewing in the loaded silence.)

Back arches tall, instead of its usual relaxed hunch. "D'you think I'm not used to being stabbed here, huh?

I've had the likes of you carrying knives, bottles, all sorts."

"You think you're the backbone."

Nose tries intervening but Right Hand unclenches for a second and taps the side of Nose. "Keep out of it."

Left Ear is cocked in the direction of the fracas and Right Hand's fist clenches tighter again. "As for you Ears – you deserve a good boxing – wigging all the time!"

The boxing begins and Left Ear suddenly loses all sound. They were big blows. Stunned, and red-raw, Left Ear tries to shake off the temporary deafness. Don't the other Body Parts realize how precious sound is? How primaeval?

Right Hand is called to the Diary Room.

Half an hour later it comes out, its fingers stroking Left Ear in contrition. Then Right Hand starts gathering up its belongings: nail files, nail polish, creams, lotions, all disappear into its handbag.

Left Ear cocks itself questioningly towards Right Hand.

"I'm being evicted from the Big Mother Body," Right Hand signals. "Big Mother doesn't tolerate any violence between her Body Parts and I've infringed that rule."

The Eyes come over, weeping. "Oh, you're not being thrown out, Right Hand. Everyone makes mistakes."

Right Hand wipes away the tears from both Eyes. (Right Hand can be so gentle and comforting if treated right. They all have their other sides. But especially the Hands, and the Eyes. Mouth too. Though Left Ear knows that too many different sides and moods can lead to the downfall of Body Parts.)

Later that evening, Right Hand, all beautifully painted and bedecked with bangles, is sent on its way by fellow Body Parts. It waves goodbye majestically, and the Eyes sob again, Nose sniffs.

The following day, Big Mother announces the results of this week's Nominations. "The Body Parts up for nomination this week are – in no particular order– "

(Big pause from Big Mother)

"Brain."

(Another pause from Big Mother)

"And Heart."

They all hang on, wondering if there's to be another Body Part in the firing line, but it seems that Big Mother has completed this week's revelation.

Mouth drops open a good few inches. "I'm shocked! I really am! I had one of you down to win it!"

"We all did." The Eyes are twin reflectors of disbelief. (Big Mother likes twins). "An absolute travesty."

Left Ear hears all the comments, spoken or otherwise. It's obvious what's happened. A large number of Body Parts have been nominating tactically, voting out the likely winners that pose the greatest threat, just for a bit of short-lived glory, a bit of self-advancement, or maybe to promote the cause of some poor forgotten Body Part.

It's an agonizingly long wait until Friday, the day when it'll be curtains for either Brain or Heart.

Left Ear tries to listen beyond the beat of Heart, trying to gauge its state as a result of the news.

Listen to your heart. Heart sounds heavy. The Eyes are picking up on it, you only have to listen to the water falling from them. Heart must be feeling cold and rejected. What Body is it that can give up its heart?

But what about Brain? Brain is more than rational. Brain is everything. Which Body Part thinks it can function without Brain? What foolish Parts are these when separated from one another?

On Friday evening, as is customary, all Body Parts sit around on the Big Mother sofa waiting to hear the voice of the outside adjudicator.

"Good evening Big Mother Body. This is Nadiva."

"Good evening, Nadiva."

"The results have now been counted and verified and I can now reveal that the next Body Part to leave the Big Mother Body will be– "

(Big pause, plus nervous anticipation from many of the Body Parts, including those not up for nomination)

"– Heart."

A gasp from Mouth.

A reddening of both Ears.

Both Eyes filling up.

As Heart goes to prepare for its big exit, gathering up its veins, its blood supplies, and all it brought into the Big Mother Body, Left Ear hears the thought: *A body ruled by heart is better than a body ruled by head.* But the people have spoken and it's Heart that leaves tonight. The rest of the Body Parts send Heart into the outside world in whatever way each knows. The Big Mother Body opens her chest for a moment, the crowd are calling for Heart, calling for its very blood, they sacrificed it for the Head, and now they have it. It is all theirs, pumping away. It is all theirs, full of emotion.

Inside the heartless Big Mother Body, Brain now rules, unopposed.

STARS

Cranleigh

First port of call on itinerary, for possibility of inclusion in our travel guide.

Bears little resemblance to picture in brochure of sunny white town house with hanging baskets. Am all for dropping one of its three stars already: trailing petunia more a withered bracken in real life; whitewash of exterior more a gull-grey.

Andy reminds me of First Law: don't rate a B&B by its cover, but by its breakfasts. First Law says it's not just how they do the mushrooms and tomatoes or the amount they give; it's whether they offer variety (different combinations every day, good choice of items etc). It's whether they say, "what would you like for your breakfast this morning?" rather than you having to make up your mind the night before when you don't always know how you'll be feeling the next day (especially on the back of a rough night). Some mornings you might not want cooked breakfast at all.

Remind Andy that breakfast is only one third of the equation; that the bed bit comes before the breakfast. And before the bed comes the host.

Hover with luggage outside Cranleigh, preparing to meet our host who could still redeem himself and win back lost star. Sounded pretty jolly on the blower, didn't he?

Get a 3 star welcome from Greg, though one of his stars is winking on and off by end of initial tour. Greg a bit in-your-face. In-*my*-face, rather, me being female.

Doesn't give Andy much eye contact. Shows us first to our own separate lounge downstairs. Did have high hopes that 'own separate lounge' would make up for lack of 'own separate loo'. Feel first stages of disappointment setting in. Had imagined separate lounge to be off our bedroom but this lounge completely separate. On a different floor, to be precise. Makes it seem like residents' lounge, without the other residents.

Follow Greg up to our room. Room bright and clean but no kettle or tea tray in sight. Decide I can't be looking in right places but thorough eyeballing of room doesn't bring them into vision. Didn't think to check for the cup symbol denoting teas & coffees in all rooms. Assumed everywhere has them these days, especially 3 star establishments. Check cupboards in case tray of beverage sachets hidden away. Few minutes later check lounge (assuming kettle and drinks must be down here). Return upstairs incredulous. Andy points out note on door: teas & coffees on request. Greg didn't mention this in his spiel. Decide Greg doesn't want us bothering him for a cuppa.

Later, after fish & chip sit-down meal in town, do bother Greg for hot drink. Think a) it's cold out and b) we're paying for hospitality. Sit in 'own separate lounge' for duration of hot drink before telling Andy I'm off upstairs to our room because TV lounge not cosy and looks grim at night with dark carpet and no curtains to draw over windows. Windows add insult to injury giving ringside view into Greg's kitchen, stocked with state-of-the-art kettle, hot beverages on tap, biscuits in airtight jars, probably bought by Mrs Greg (so far heard but not seen).

Another couple of stars drop during awful night's kip due largely to poor ergonomics, i.e. bed below window. Freeze in bed, despite Andy crashed out on other side.

Think to myself: hot drinks could have staved off chill of September nights. Feel around in wardrobe for extra blankets. Hands touch bare wood. Never known place without extra blankets. Feel around for jumper and bedsocks instead. Cold takes its toll on bladder (in spite of paucity of liquid refreshment), resulting in traipse to shared loo on landing. Notice window on landing open, duly slam it shut. Rattle handle of bathroom (why isn't the bugger opening?) Hear plumbing noises sounding suspiciously reminiscent of someone in shower. Realize it's later than I thought. Rattle and stomp some more till hunky guy emerges from bathroom with wet hair and nothing on but towel. Shiver and pee and return for two miserable hours of sleep, dreaming of hot water bottles.

At breakfast (in our own separate lounge) Greg asks how we slept. Get in before Andy comes up with polite, played-down version and tell Greg in no uncertain terms about cold night, pointedly turning gas fire on full. Greg (in shirt sleeves) looks at me oddly. Unperturbed, ask Greg re central heating as mentioned in guide (denoted by CH symbol.) Greg makes a lot of fuss about having to turn individual radiators on in each room. "It's only September, after all!" Comes up with solution of blankets and fan heater. Made to feel foolish. While Greg preparing cooked part of our breakfasts – full English for Andy; tomatoes, mushrooms, toast for me – look out on peaceful garden with pleasing flowers, bench, and fish pond. Certain there was picture of flower in the key too, denoting access to garden for residents, though Greg not mentioned this either. Say to Andy, "That's it. We'll move on today instead of making do another night." Andy again reminds me of First Law. A B&B can always redeem itself by its breakfasts. Thank Andy for the reminder. Have fruit juice and cereal. Choice and range of cereals at least 3 star. My tea and Andy's coffee OK, though need weightlifter to pick up teapot. Cooked bit of my breakfast probably 2 star. Good, but not outstanding. Come to most important bit of breakfast: toast and marmalade. Decide this is what I'm really judging. Greg commits cardinal sin. Toast in English B&B should be white, arrive in a rack and be slightly chewy. Should be cold enough for butter not to melt and topped with golden shredded marmalade. Instead Greg's toast warm, with butter already spread and melting by the time it reaches our table. Feel like an infant or someone incapable of spreading own butter (surprised Greg didn't cut toast into soldiers to boot). Whole breakfast now sub-standard. Am about to tell Andy all stars should be dropped for this unforgivable error alone when Greg makes comment re TV, here in our Own Separate Lounge. "Did you know leaving a television on standby uses up more electricity than switching it off?"

Want to wipe smile off G's skinflint face.

Upstairs, couple of heavy-duty blankets and fan heater have been rustled up by G's other half. Decide it's too little too late.

Compare notes with Andy. He's for keeping all three of G's stars. Say to A, "Over my dead body. G is a one-star man and that's being generous."

Feel my rating is fully justified. One-star men don't give you teas & coffees on tap and they spread it a bit thin. One-star men are skinflints, saving on warmth and electricity at every opportunity (though he did have a friendly smile).

Leave Greg's with lame excuse, produced by Andy (I'd have told G the truth). Find myself wondering what star rating I'd give Andy (he rarely brings me up a cuppa in the morning and keeps himself warm with extra jerseys).

Sunnymead

At 5 pm arrive at Sunnymead Guest House on spec, after day of sightseeing and driving. Sunnymead = 3 star double-fronted establishment on high street leading to sea front. Advertizing vacancies. Looks promising. Woman in slippers we take to be live-in chambermaid answers door. Soon discover lady in question is proprietor. (Don't like to be ageist but did look a bit too old to be chambermaid.) Ask if she's got any rooms en suite (having briefed, begged and bullied Andy that a loo on the landing is out of the question). Forget to mention teas & coffees but decide we'd have to be v unlucky to come across another host with Greg's rare malady. In spite of appearance proprietor gives us 4 star welcome. Have you travelled far? Was your journey OK? Do you need help with your luggage? Guests like hosts to get that balance between taking an interest and giving them personal space, i.e. to come and go as they please. Our host passes the host bit of three-pronged test with flying colours. Next prong, the bedroom. Smell of cooked breakfast still on the air as we're led up patterned stairs to Room 1. Our host holds up key in her hand. "This is for the front door." Takes hold of other key on ring and shows us bit of green plastic to distinguish it from first key. Puts bedroom key in lock of Room 1, talking us through complicated instructions of turns and half-turns and the lock can be a bit stiff, so be assertive with it. Realize brain's dead from sightseeing and travel – hope Andy's taking it in.

Door opens on room with fussy dark green pattern on yellow walls (green bits made of flock) making room look dingy, though lending character. Think to myself, Gloomymead. Bedspread navy and flowery, not coordinating with walls at all. Observe smell on air of flannels and sweat, disguised by air freshener. Our host draws our attention to free-standing shower in room (shape not unlike public phone box of the obsolete variety). Phone box with a dress, I later say to Andy, referring to frilly green shower curtain. Realize phone box is probably cause of smell permeating atmosphere. Host opens other door onto en suite. Follow her in one at a time. En suite literally a bog – (sink keeping shower company in room). Bog very bog-standard, grim yellow paintwork on walls, pipes in evidence. Room not doing well in stars department so far. Subject of breakfast is broached – times, what's on offer etc. Our host draws our attention to TV which needs £1 coins. £1 equals three and a half hours' viewing time approx. Need to pick Andy's gob up off the floor, mine catching up rapidly. Maybe too hard on skinflint Greg.

Only daylight in room coming through window set far back in recess. Distinct feeling if could see out of window, would overlook bins and barrels. After our host is gone, discover long pole and impress Andy with twisting window open and shut. Open bedside drawer and jump back in surprise to discover hairdryer next to Bible. A few leaflets of local attractions on top of dressing table near tea tray. A tea tray – alleluia! Check tray for teas & coffees. As usual never enough milks. Not even creams or powder milks to make do when proper milks run out. Only four between us meaning A & I having to share milks for each of our four drinks throughout day: 1) before breakfast 2) late afternoon 3) mid-evening 4) bedtime. Say to A: typical 2 star approach, skimping on the milks. Decide we can always purloin extra milks from cafés during day. Can't complain too much, at least a step up from Greg's non-existent tea tray. Try out TV. Picture terrible. Green and wavering. After meal in town, come back to watch TV in TV lounge to save on TV money in room. Fitful night's sleep ensues. In wakeful phases take peek at night sky on way to bog. Think profound thoughts befitting the hour re stars in the sky – if a star collapses, a singularity is inevitable. Let ideas incubate and fuse and come up with new Law: if a star collapses then a single room is uninhabitable. Marvel at my capacity for the burlesque until cold light of day brings me back down to earth.

Gloomymead redeemed by 9 am breakfast. Cheerios, followed by fried egg, grilled toms, Linda McCartney sausages, baked beans, mushrooms & waffles. Forgot to say to host, no eggs please. Reason: eggs constipate, though constipation counteracted by beans. Don't like fried eggs especially, hate yolk running cold all over plate, would have had scrambled eggs if not constipating. Realize my fault entirely – our host would have obliged. Instead, Andy gets unexpected extra fried egg belly-flopping into his toms when host disappearing into kitchen with other guests' plates. White chewy toast gets my 3 stars.

My rating:

Host ***
Bedroom *
Breakfast ***

Overall rating (mine) **
Overall rating (Andy's) ***

The Four Seasons

Turn up at pre-booked Four Seasons Guest House, Sunday 5 pm.
Four Seasons has 4 stars twinkling our welcome. A star for all seasons.
Exterior of Victorian house even better than brochure. Sun blazing on steps up to entrance. Chairs and sunshade in front garden. Potted plants in doorway. Sign saying 'no vacancies' under swinging Four Seasons sign. Good sign. Eagerly await 4 star reception. Mrs Dobbs, our host, looks promising. Delivers all right phrases. Seems to have got balance just right between too in-your-face and too unavailable. Shows us little boxes in dining room for us to help ourselves to extra milks, teas etc. Thumbs up to Mrs Dobbs for catering for the likes of us. Shows us fruit bowl where we can help ourselves to fruit (though imagine us being too polite and British). 4 star establishments have those little extras – the personal touch. Find myself asking: does Andy have the personal touch? Does he give me enough teas & coffees? Does he come en suite or do I need to book in somewhere else for daily personal needs? Wonder how many stars Andy would give me. Decide he'd give me more than I'd give him.
Room immaculate: warm, bright, with free TV, plus en suite with bath, sink and coloured towels. Think, this is more like it. Tea tray with variety of teas, including herbal, milks aplenty. Will probably not need to avail ourselves of extras downstairs but nice to know they're there. Tin of homemade biscuits, next to packet biscuits. Place too good to be true. Mrs Dobbs mentions breakfast and draws our attention to printed sheets with choice of

breakfasts & times. Asks us to leave our sheets down in lobby by nine o'clock tonight. Decide this is where it all falls down, too impersonal and reminiscent of hospitals. Look at printed sheets after Mrs Dobbs leaves us to own devices. Range of times: 7.30-9.30 am. Think, 9.30 am v civilized and not often an option. Gets my vote. Tick tea, white bread, and veggie breakfast, deleting items I don't fancy: egg (too constipating), beans (too much the other way) and fried bread (too greasy), leaving tomato, hash brown, and mushroom. In the singular. After 4 star night's sleep and melon chunks for first bit of breakfast, see that cooked bit of breakfast is very literal. One hash brown, one tomato, one mushroom, plus plenty of white plate. Think to myself, if it were me, I'd give a couple each of hash browns, mushrooms, and tomatoes, so they don't look lost on plate.

Stay in Four Seasons another couple of days. Clean towels and linen every day. A and I not agreeing on star ratings of any of our visited establishments so far. Shows widening gulf between us. Conclude A has whole different concept of what's acceptable, what's good, what's excellent. A over-generous with stars, me stingy. Realize we're not entirely compatible, though A thinks we are. I rest my case. He doesn't rest his. Not his pillow case anyway. Pummels me with 4 star pillow. A pillow fight ensues, resulting in A cracking his nut against walls with superior sound-proofing. Says he's seeing stars. The feminine in me rubs his nut better, then his nuts, leading to 2 star sex, i.e. functional, acceptable sex, but of limited range. Realize better quality services probably on offer elsewhere, but keep coming back to the 2 star man, year after year.

Nine months later give birth to 5 star baby (4 of mine, 1 of Andy's). Know I'm 4 star cause have plenty of milk for drinks throughout day. Know baby is 4 star – comes with huge en suite, immaculate laundry, own personal chambermaid, and the personal touch. (What should we do today? Shall I carry you up the stairs?)

Gaze at baby. Now know what's meant by: you're a star.

KARMIC BREW

"I think we've met before," says Noel in the pink vest and striped calico trousers as Julie decorates her plate with a few of the awesome delicacies from the trestle table. Bring food to share, it said on the flyer advertizing today's healing workshop of Surinder's, and everyone else has gone to town with their contributions. Home-made quiches and huge bowls of salad with olives and avocado and their own wooden salad servers, what's more. Julie watched, daunted, a few moments ago, as the vegan woman with the purple knotted scarf on her head peeled off the cling film from her two terrines and rolled both pieces into one ball. That one's lentil and chick pea pâté, said the vegan woman, and that's plum quinoa – all organic and GM free. They're popular too, everyone's trying them, while Julie's packet of Mr Kipling cakes are still sealed in their box.

"I feel as if I know you from somewhere." Noel is staring at Julie with those lustrous blue eyes above the beard. "You've been feeling it too, haven't you?"

Yes, she has noticed how loving and trusting everyone is here; how easy it is to feel on a deeper level with them straight away. Bags and valuables are left unattended (not that she's got anything of value to speak of), and you only have to look around to see demonstrations of unconditional acceptance, like those two angel-faced ladies in their fifties, rocking together in a lingering hug. It seems the hug has crossed the Atlantic.

Earlier today, the group concentrated on transforming something negative in their lives into something positive: in Julie's case, her gloomy money situation. It does grind her down, never being able to afford life's little luxuries and she shared her hopes for a holiday in Cornwall. Nothing grand, but her friend has got this cottage in a cove with views of fishing boats and shiny black rocks. She hasn't been able to afford a holiday for donkey's years she told the group – (she even had to save up just to afford to pay the concessionary £20 for today's workshop, though she didn't mention that part) – and all she needs is the £50 train fare down to her dream cottage...

The universe will always provide, said one of the Angel Faces, stroking the rosy quartz crystal at her bosom. You just have to ask it, put your faith in it. The other Angel, the one in floaty blue chiffon, said, Do some positive affirmations, my dear. Don't block wealth, money is just another energy, at which point the vegan woman's nine-year-old boy, called Kern, said, Money makes the world go round, doesn't it, mummy, and his mother stroked his back between his shoulder blades.

"We've met in a previous life, Julie," says Noel. "That's where I know you from."

So many of these people have such unusual names. Kern's mother is called Willow. I chose it for myself after my initiation at the sweat lodge, she told Julie earlier. Julie smiled, not fully understanding, but thought it a super idea, calling yourself after a pretty tree. Maybe she should do it too, instead of sticking with plain old Julie. And then there's Surinder himself, the workshop coordinator, who, though he doesn't look Indian, certainly has an air of the Indian about him. The slight inflection to some of his phrases, the tied-back white hair billowing to his waist, the embroidered shirt, the talk about particles vibrating at different frequencies and how love and light can transform these particles – love from the Godhead. She doesn't understand the technical side of it but Surinder must know what he's talking about because he has a large following and a guru called Jayashankar, though she only found out all this today, and he's got lots of books and CDs for sale which most of the others have scrutinized and swooned over before heaping their notes and coins in a beautiful pot engraved with the lotus flower. At least, one of the Angels said they were lotus flowers. A symbol of rebirth, did she say?

"In fact we've lived several lifetimes together, Julie," says Noel. "I think we've been karmically related since Egyptian times."

"Have we? Really?" Julie looks at him wide-eyed. She feels special and important in a way she's never felt before.

"Yes," says Noel, who isn't bad-looking. "You get a feel for these things when you've done a lot of past life regression."

Julie finds a dog hair in her pâté, and leaves the rest of it. She longs for Pringles. Her throat feels tight, her legs weak and her head is starting to ache with all the intense soul-searching of the morning. She wonders whether she should nip off to the loo and take some Anadin but that would be cheating, she would feel an entire fraud. Anyway Noel is watching her, concerned. "There's a massage bed in the meditation room, Julie. I can give you some craniosacral therapy in a bit...when your food's gone down."

How considerate everyone is. Cranial...she didn't quite catch...Cranial Sacred did he say? It certainly sounds good whatever it is. She's not tried many of these new therapies herself and it's got to beat Anadin.

Presently, she lies down on the massage bed, face upwards, and makes herself comfortable. Before he gets the Cranium doodah underway, Noel asks her if she's been feeling ill.

"Well yes," she says, amazed. "I have actually." He's

psychic, she knew it. He must be right about the past lives too.

"In what way?"

"Headache...constricted throat...a bit dizzy."

Noel is nodding knowingly. "I thought so. Do you often have problems with your throat?"

"Sometimes."

"I'm getting this memory..."

"Really?"

He's waving a crystal above her throat, a different colour than the Angel's, a sort of blue. "Aquamarine for the throat chakra," says Noel. "I'm just seeing in which direction it swings..."

"What's it saying?"

"Mmm, it's as I thought. A blockage from a past life...I think you were garrotted."

"Garrotted? Really?"

"It's OK. I can do some past life healing on it." She falls into silence as Noel gets to work on the cranial fluids and subtle tides around her body, something like that. She hardly feels a thing, except a gentle touch on her temples and the odd bit of light pressure under her neck and back. When his head is above hers, she smells garlic, not from his mouth which is closed, but coming through his nostrils. Occasionally he makes strange gurgly noises.

After a while, which might be one minute or ten, Noel says, "Feeling any better?"

She gives a puzzled nod, though it's a lie. The truth is her head is more muzzy, her throat more inflamed, but she doesn't ponder it further because she's just heard the clanking of buckets followed by an apparition with a mop of black hair peering through the glass in the door. "Was that one of ours?" she croaks.

Noel shrugs. "Just concentrate on blue light, Julie.

And the sacred mantra Ham." He seems to be stroking and patting the air above her body.

She closes her eyes and wonders about garrottings, quickly turning her thoughts to her dream holiday instead: sea waves breaking tall, lobster pots, seagulls nestling in yellowing tin mines, and when she next looks up, most of the group has reassembled in the meditation room on the horseshoe of chairs.

Noel leads her to a chair next to his and Surinder begins the afternoon session with a relaxation exercise, breathing in for four, breathing out for eight. The males make loud exhalation noises, and then Surinder takes them all on a guided meditation. During the long silence when they're supposed to be deeply relaxed and seeing images of healing light particles, picturing them as stars or angels, Julie feels herself to be deeply tense, her face aflame. It was hard enough doing the one-to-one healing with Noel but here it's like being on stage, in a performance, only you have to remember your silence instead of your words. She can't stop swallowing, or thinking of swallowing, or the creak in her chair, or wanting to scratch the tip of her nose which has sprung an untimely itch. What if she should burst out laughing? Eventually she subsides into her own imaginings of a wide Cornish bay with waves breaking in frills before rolling in. She tries visualizing the fifty pounds for the train fare. Imagine your purse bursting with notes, said the chiffon Angel; picture yourself, rich and extravagant, sitting on that train. How good it must feel to master the same spiritual heights as these veterans, she thinks, as she tries her hardest to attend to the CD that's now playing softly, with haunting little clicks of whales to tie in with Surinder's imagery.

All of a sudden there's a great clatter. Like the sound of someone tripping over a chair, and some words, gruff against the whales. Julie dares to open an eye though everyone else seems to be the picture of yogic serenity, their eyes still closed, their hands loose but positioned carefully in their laps as Surinder has instructed them.

"Sounds like a load of fuckin doors creaking," says one of the new arrivals to his mate as he topples onto a seat. He's got a shock of black hair and a leather jacket and, in spite of his attempts to whisper, his words are loud, and thick with the north of England. The other smaller man beside him titters and mutters. He is thin and older, with straggles of grey hair.

Surinder closes the meditation and smiles at the newcomers while the other participants stretch and gradually return to their present surroundings. "Welcome," says Surinder, and invites the two men to take off their shoes and leave them just inside the door. "If you don't mind my smelly socks," says the black leathers, unlacing his huge, mud-encrusted boots and hauling them off his heels. Julie smiles inwardly because the small meditation room already smells faintly of feet. The older man remains shod, his arms folded in rebellion across his breastbone.

Surinder suggests another round of names. "I'm Brew," says the black leathers when it's his turn. "This is me mate Billy."

"You have to put some money in the pot next-door," says Kern.

"Well we can sort that out later," says Surinder. "As you've only come for half a day, I'm sure we can arrange a small reduction."

The two men look confused, as though Surinder has just spoken to them in Sanskrit or Urdu, and then Kern looks up at his mother and says, "Money makes the world go round, doesn't it, mummy?"

"So does booze if you have enough of the fuckin

stuff," laughs Brew, taking out a can of beer from the interior tunnels of his jacket. "Round and round." Surinder's disciples look on uneasily as Brew snaps it open, takes a swig and waves it questioningly at one or two other members of the circle, before handing it to the mumbling grey Billy. At this juncture one of the Angels clears her throat in a way which makes Julie wonder whether she's also had problems with past life garrottings. "We must concentrate on helping Julie to attract money energy into her life," says the Angel. "So she can go and stay in the apartment by the sea." (Perhaps she is American after all).

"Trust in the universe," says her Angel sister, lifting her rosy crystal to her lips. "The universe will always provide," and it reminds Julie of something else. The Lord is bountiful perhaps.

There are sighs and slightly obscene-sounding consonants slurring from the old grey rebel who has dark teeth like bars across his mouth.

"Julie's still got some karmic debt to pay off around money," says Noel, ignoring any underlying unpleasantries. "At lunchtime Julie and I discovered we've been through several lifetimes together…and Julie's chosen poverty for whatever lessons her soul needs to learn in this incarnation."

Have I? thinks Julie, but her head is really hammering now, her face taking turns between cerise and bleach.

One of the Angels looks at Noel, intrigued. "Can you tell a person's past life just by being in their company?"

"I can usually feel it, yes."

"What a gift."

Brew gives a cynical laugh. "What about my past life then?"

"Well, I'm definitely picking up some Viking energy…" says Noel.

"No," protests Brew. "When I was a little lad? A teenager? They're me past lives, aren't they?" Noel hesitates and Brew says to Billy, "That's him fucked, ain't it?"

At this point, and not before time in the view of some participants who are annoyed at having their post-meditation highs brought so abruptly back down to earth, Surinder steers them back to the content of the workshop: the Healing Particles and the Great White Light. Panels of sun beam down through the upper windows as people feed back on their meditation experiences, until Brew cuts across talk of etheric bodies with "Ey Billy lad, any of them sarnies left? I'm fuckin starving." He then reaches into his leathers. "Oh hang on. You're all right. They're in here." He pulls out a squashed Hovis bag and starts munching on a doorstep while Kern, seated in the next chair, can't take his eyes off him. "Want a bite, kid?" says Brew, oblivious to the blue chiffon Angel who's putting a finger vertically against her lips in a stealthy shush. "Here, have a whole one."

"Thank you." Kern tucks into the thick slab offered him. After a few bites he starts to dismember it, wondering at its alien contents. Suddenly, Willow, who until now was paying close attention to Surinder's pearls of wisdom, lets out a horrified shriek. "Urk, ham!" She pulls out a cling film ball from her bag and starts unravelling it. "Here, spit it out into this, Kern!" She bangs his back between his shoulder blades until he coughs it up.

"He was fuckin enjoying that, weren't you, kid?" says Brew, nudging Kern in the ribs who grins from ear to red ear.

And then the Chiffon Angel stands up, appearing a lot less cherubic now. "Look, these constant interruptions are most discourteous to Surinder who's travelled miles to be with us here today." There are nods of assent, and, except for the intermittent private murmurings of Billy, all is calm for a while.

Julie meanwhile thinks about her Mr Kipling cakes, still unopened next-door on the trestle table. At least they're not alone in getting the seal of disapproval – Brew's ham sandwiches have been given the definite thumbs-down. She sees that she'll probably have to take them home again though she doesn't know when she'll next feel like eating them. Her appetite's gone for a Burton and her symptoms are still raging. She feels she's let herself down. She came here today in the hope of realizing her dream; of finding the key to vibrant energy and wealth. Earlier in the day it felt as if she was making a real breakthrough but now her throat is getting more taut, her head more painful, her body weaker. She clings desperately to the chair to stop herself fainting.

"You all right, luv?"

She looks up and realizes Brew is talking to her.

"She had some karmic healing at lunch time." Noel is now standing behind her protectively, his hands on her temples. She's right under his cloud of garlic which is making her feel nauseous, along with everything else. "Sometimes we feel worse for a while as our bodies get rid of the toxins…"

Fckkkkshhht. Billy groans his dissent.

"You know, it's your sort who give men a bad name," says Noel. "Coming in here with your aggressive manner. You want to get in touch with your yin side," and then one of the rescuing Angels clears her throat again and peers in on Julie. "You've done a lot of heady stuff today, dear," she says. "But don't worry. The body will heal itself. Isn't that so?" Her question is directed at Surinder. "We're all self-regulating, like little Gaias," says Surinder, with more than a hint of Mombai. "The human body, like the earth, has a mechanism for healing itself of all harm."

"Bollocks," says Billy, now fully exposing the decaying bars in his mouth which let through too much tongue, before his speech deteriorates into another string of incomprehensibles. "That's a good fuckin point, Billy lad," says Brew. "People are dying of cancer every day."

"We all have the potential for eternal life." Surinder is still utterly self-composed and full of the Godhead particles. "There's a man in India..."

More probable obscenities are uncorked from Billy, while Willow shakes her head. "I've had enough of this. I don't know how other people are feeling."

"Hear hear," says Noel, turning to the two intruders. "We don't want you here. You're disturbing the whole healing process."

"Hasn't done much for her," says Brew, waving his can in the direction of Julie.

"As I've already explained," says Noel. "Julie's system is detoxifying itself of poisons. Only you were just too blitzed to hear the first time."

"Poisons my fuckin arse. She's got that flu that's going round, ain't it, Billy?"

"Look, we've had enough of your drunken gibberish," says Noel, trying to tip Brew from his chair. "Just get lost."

"Get your fuckin hands off my chair," says Brew but most of the group is behind Noel, except Surinder who is practising Supreme Detachment, and the Crystal Angel who says maybe they've attracted Brew and Billy here this afternoon; that perhaps there's a lesson somewhere for the group as a whole.

"Come on, Billy." Brew is staggering to his feet and giving Billy a helping hand. A slop of beer escapes as he tilts his can in the direction of Noel and looks over at

Julie. "I should watch him, luv. He's just trying to get his rocks off."

"OUT!" Noel's face has turned purple and an irate vein has appeared in his neck. Brew clambers back into the immense boots, laces them haphazardly, and calls back to Julie. "D'you want us to phone you a cab, luv? 'Ere hold me tin, Billy, while I phone a cab for Jules."

Noel gives him a final shove through the door.

After a few moments, while the group resumes its composure, relieved to be detoxified of their uninvited guests and purifying the negative energies with pine incense, Julie sways out after them. They're right, she probably has got the flu, and she does want a taxi; she can't possibly walk home in this state.

She catches up with Brew and Billy outside, sitting on the wall. "We'll wait till your cab comes, luv," says Brew. "Eh, take some of the white pills and get your head down when you get home. Brew's orders."

"Thanks, I will." She's feeling better already since she stepped into the fresh air. "What made you both come to the workshop anyway?"

"Thought it was that No To War talk thingy, didn't we? Must have got the wrong fuckin day or room!"

Julie smiles and turns out her pocket. "Sixty eight pence. Not enough for a taxi."

"Behave," says Brew, stuffing a bundle of tenners into her hand. "We found the lucky jackpot today, didn't we Billy lad?"

He takes a swig of beer and winks at her as the taxi pulls up. "Just call it your karmic pay-off."

HEADBOARDS

Not everyone who places ads in personal columns is a saddo.

Take me. A successful Love Consultant by profession, being paid a king's ransom to sort out their affairs of the heart, but until the ad I had no love life to call my own. It was the old tale of doctor heal thyself: too busy sorting out everyone else's love lives and no time left for my own. An ad in a personal column would be the ultimate time-saver, I decided. It would not only exploit my knowledge of human behaviour but also get straight to the moot point of the bedroom. If worded carefully, if placed in the right outlet and reaching my target audience (those newspaper readers within a reasonably mature age range) it would generate replies aplenty, and the only demands on my time: the selection of a shortlist.

I knew my ad would need to a) stand out from the crowd and b) cut all the downstairs-hall-and-landings crap and get straight to the bedroom. Having shared the beds of various men and women in previous relationships, I felt myself well equipped with some valuable insights. Not least: judge the lover by the headboard. With this in mind I set about composing my ad:

Attractive professional lady, young 49, wltm either gender for fun and saucy nights in. Photo of your headboard guarantees my reply.

My ad ran for two weeks in a national, c/o my own personal Box Number in said national, and I received a staggering nine replies: seven men, two women. I discarded two from the off: both male and both omitting that all-important photo, though I have to say they mainly failed on other counts – one with his abysmal attempts to be mysterious, the other with his obvious mental health issues. Another photoless letter invited me to visit his website and view his headboards. I did, it turned out to be some online shopping outfit specializing in bedroom furniture. His letter had contained the message, *I can guarantee you will be wowed by my headboards.* I wasn't, and he was duly binned along with the other two.

Which left me with six headboards (well, five to be exact – but more about that in a moment.) I'd promised to reply to all who'd included photos which, I realized with hindsight, wasn't so prudent. I looked at the snap of Pine with Spindles, at his equally spindly handwriting, his words separated with the same amount of spacing. No, I didn't want to meet Pine with Spindles in spite of his promises of *passion unfettered* and *hours of fun.* I just had this sinking feeling about him which counts for a lot in this field. I didn't want to waste either of our time by replying. Pine is the sort you marry, spindles or no spindles. Not the racy sort.

I promised myself I'd meet the rest, even though their letters didn't always match the personality of the headboard. Sometimes there was no letter at all as in the case of the leopard skin headboard in the shape of a big heart. Just a name and number and *hope to hear from you* on the back of the photo. I tried Tiger Heart's mobile several times with a view to fixing a meeting but I always got her Orange voicemail. I put her on the back burner, I had my others to work through.

My curiosity had been aroused by the only other letter on my shortlist which didn't contain a photo. But this one wasn't trying to be mysterious. *Hi there – sorry, I haven't got a headboard, but I hope that won't count against me because you sound like a fun lady and I'm sure we could have lots of that.* It got me wondering: what sort of a guy has no headboard? There had to be loads, thinking about it. The poor, the young, futon fanatics, and those who simply slept in a bed without a headboard. No Headboard had to be a student, I was convinced. *Hi there.* That sounded kinda studenty. He hadn't enclosed his phone number so I couldn't speak to the guy until I met him and oh dear. On the wrong side of eighty, toothless, and wearing slippers. I looked at his bed; little more than a glorified camp bed. "Sit down," he said, patting the stained blanket beside him. We exchanged names and talked mainly about benefits that he might, would, should be entitled to. I felt like his nurse or a volunteer from Age Concern. When I got up to go he clasped my long black hair and then my hand. "Can I kiss you?" he said. I offered my cheek and felt something cold and damp brush against it. Just as I opened the door he said, "Same time tomorrow then?" I blew him a kiss goodbye and left.

A humbling experience, proving to me that I still had a lot to learn about the psychology of headboards.

Meanwhile I focussed my attention on Padded & Buttoned, wondering what on earth had possessed me to include such a ghastly headboard in my final selection. It looked like something for the over sixties, something your Aunt Flo might have and, on closer inspection, appeared to be a headboard for a single bed. It had to be a wind-up. Then I reread her letter, reminding me that it was her wit and humour that had saved her from immediate oblivion. "I will take the bored out of headboard," she'd written. She'd also joked about Padded & Buttoned, assuring me that fun could be had on such a bed.

You will have gathered by now that the person and their headboard were fast becoming synonymous and when I went to meet Padded & Buttoned at her flat for the first time, I was aware that not one single erotic moment had yet taken place with any of my prospectives, nor looked likely to.

Padded & Buttoned was about twenty-eight, with an accent I couldn't place. "Come through, come through," she said, taking me to her bedroom. "This is said headboard, come and meet her!" She stroked it, moving her fair fingers over the buttons like they were nipples. "She's lovely and soft, come and feel!" She made me look at Padded & Buttoned in a totally new light; furthermore she, too, knew something of the psychology of headboards, albeit in a populist sort of way. "I love a soft headboard, I do, because I'm soft in the head, they tell me, soft by day, but solid and stiff with hairspray at night. That's me. I think you should have a different headboard for every mood, don't you?" We lay together fully clothed on Padded & Buttoned and for a brief moment I could imagine fun and frolics happening for the first time since I'd started out on this venture. But I realized that my interest in her was strictly mental; her thoughts on headboards were fascinating and would be useful to me at some stage (when I got round to writing the definitive book on the subject) but in a physical sense she wasn't doing it for me. Her headboard hadn't lied. "I'll let you know," I said to her, like your typical rotten interviewer. "I've still got other people to see." (Not a word of a lie).

"Well, it's been lovely meeting you anyway." She scooped up a Scottie-type dog which had just emerged from another room (probably her Aunt Flo's). "And if you want to get to know my headboard more intimately, you know where we are."

I wasn't doing too well. Still no returned call from Tiger Heart, but Black Rails beckoned. This was probably the most evocative headboard of the lot: a huge imposing thing with hard black rails, the wall behind a stark white. This guy was into pain, giving or receiving. I knew him before I met him – thirty-two, covered in tattoos, an ex-con unable to shake off the bars – falling, as I was, into the same populist trap as Padded & Buttoned and therefore quite unprepared for the podgy and bald fifty-something I was ultimately faced with. But it didn't matter to me, the headboard was bigger than the man. He didn't waste time with social niceties, he took me straight to his piece de resistance and as there was nothing else in his bleak little room to distract me, nothing on the white walls, the bed loomed large and all-encompassing. I had little choice but to focus on the imposing black rails, on those formidable black posts at either side. They were crying out for action. Black Rails started undoing his trousers and shirt and sat on the bed in his white vest and Y-fronts. "Will you do the honours?" Out came the handcuffs. Two pairs. One per hand. He wanted one attached to an easterly rail, the other to a westerly. We were ready to set sail on rough seas, me astride him and hanging on to the rails above him. But I didn't look at him. I just stared at that mighty headboard, gripping it and shaking it as if it were the gateway to heaven, and that was the start of my fun and games with Black Rails. He was my bit of danger: I never knew quite what to expect – usually I was the dominatrix but I also lay like a prisoner in the dungeon, quivering in awe at the overbearing fortress above.

I started dividing my time between Black Rails and Solid Wood. He was the final candidate on my shortlist, curiosity having won the day once more. Solid Wood stood out from the crowd as Black Rails had done, but unlike the almost ironic bleak of Black Rails, Solid Wood's was a desperate sort of bleak. There was a dark dinginess about the wood, like it had been the business once, sort of classy, but now you looked at it and thought junk shops. Luckily, I knew from his letter he wouldn't be another No Headboard: he was younger (in his forties), divorced, and a fellow professional. I lived and loved in hope.

I saw straightaway why he was saddled with Solid Wood: the poor man hadn't the time to replace it, same as he hadn't the time to socialize (a man after my own heart). "Tell me," I asked him on our first meeting. "What made you think I'd respond to your headboard?"

He looked at the headboard, then at me. "What's wrong with it?"

(This was worrying. If he'd said "I did it for a bit of fun" or "it was meant to be ironic" I'd have breathed a sigh of relief, but Solid Wood was deadly serious. He hadn't a clue about bedroom decorum and obviously needed some lessons in love).

Of course, I soon learned that there were pockets of passion to be found in Solid Wood; I began polishing him up nicely. He was a lot less bleak when you got to know him and he filled me in about his scientific work, every knot and grain. And it was Solid Wood – albeit indirectly – who gave me the idea of taking my Love Consultancy onto the next phase.

I was putting my stockings back on, fastening them to my basque (having successfully introduced Solid Wood to the delights of this piece of lingerie). He was tying up his shoes (we both had other appointments to keep that afternoon) when he said, "How is your thesis going?"

"Thesis?"

"You know, headboards."

"Oh you know. I'm still collecting data."

"Well, however you approach it, I'm sure you won't go in for any of this dumbed-down nonsense." He dangled his tie about his neck, crossing one side over the other. "You know the sort of thing: what your headboard says about you."

I thought of Padded & Buttoned and her soft headboard because she was "soft in the head". There was something to be said for keeping it simple. On the other hand I had to agree with him: there was a lot more to be said of the headboard. For what is a bed without its head? Just a flaccid bit of material without definition, without backdrop to late-night or early-morning thoughts. Indeed it was against Solid Wood that I thought about What Ifs. What if a Padded & Buttoned were to meet a Solid Wood? Would they get on? Would opposites attract? It could be argued that a Padded & Buttoned could do with toughening up, a solid backdrop to her evenings and mornings, while a Solid Wood might benefit from a softer covering, a more yielding nature. Or maybe like would attract like: Solid Woods and Padded & Buttoneds sticking together and never the twain meeting.

The idea was growing shoots in my head. I could expand into the whole area of Love Compatibility once the necessary studies had been carried out. I had plenty of clients on my books seeking compatible lovers; all I would require from them was a photo of their headboard which I could then match to another suitable headboard.

But I needed a bit more in the way of empirical research. I needed the help and wisdom of ordinary folk to help me with my classification of personality types. I thought of Padded & Buttoned. She probably had much to say on the subject and, caught as I was between the hard worlds of Solid Wood and Black Rails, I began to crave her softness, remembering the way she'd caressed the buttons as if they were nipples. I was convinced she wasn't as soft in the head as all that. Hadn't she said something about hardened hairspray in the evenings? About different headboards for different moods? What had made her reply to my ad in the first place?

I decided to re-establish contact with her.

"Just for a chat," I said on the phone. "I thought you might be able to help me with my research."

"I wondered when I'd hear from you again," she said and I arranged to call round at eight o'clock the following evening.

I was pleased to find her looking totally different: hair big, gothic, hard with lacquer; black dress over sheer stockings. No sign of Scottie the dog but a sultry black cat.

I told her about my Research and the Love Compatibility idea.

"You're going to play Cupid?"

"A bit ironical, I know, when I don't believe in the one perfect lover. Many imperfect ones is what keeps me ticking."

"Oh I could tell." She teased the cat's fur as she spoke. "You're not a one-lover woman."

Then she stood up and said, "Here. I've got something to show you." I followed her, watching as she put her fingers over the handle of her bedroom door and I smiled weakly as she turned it, bracing myself for another meeting with Padded & Buttoned. Instead my eyes were drawn to the lush folds of the Tiger Heart above her bed.

Before I'd had a chance to speak she said, "I'll submit to you here and now if you tell me."

"Tell you what?"

"What sort of headboard *you've* got."

I grinned. "I'll tell you afterwards."

"You promise?"

I was getting seduced by the sensual room – the red satin sheets, the open box of assorted dildos, tempting as chocolates, the come-to-bed look of the beating Tiger Heart – and I began to feel drunk with horniness. She handed me a strap-on dildo from the box which I festooned to myself, proud of its menacing profile as I strutted in front of the mirrors. In the reflection I could see that she'd found her place already, face down on the bed, her bare butt already gyrating up and down with desire. I knelt astride her, one hand steadying the dildo as I entered her, the other holding her neck down below the headboard. As I pumped her I silently intoned the words, you're not getting inside my head, you little minx, you're not, you're not! She moaned and then shrieked as we gripped and shook Tiger Heart in a paroxysm of desire. Another noise soon stopped us short. We both heard it. A crack and a snap, like bones breaking, the headboard then slipping sideways, adrift from its body, and looking suddenly pathetic and irrelevant as our lust.

"You've broken it," my bedmate said. Her voice had come over all thin and dejected, like she was passing into another mood. Like she'd lost her wild side. "You've broken my heart."

She straightened her clothes and applied some more black lipstick while I detached and wiped the dildo, carefully putting it back in its box. Then I did my best to mend her heart which seemed to be ruling her head. But she said, "I've got some more theories, you know," proving to me that her head was still engaged. "I'll tell you about them when we meet next time."

I smiled non-committally as I got up to leave, vowing there wouldn't be a next time. I made some loose arrangement to call sometime, congratulating myself on my lucky escape as I emerged onto the avenue and headed towards my car. I'm normally good at shaking off people but when she popped up at my side, I wondered whether I'd underestimated her. "Car keys," she said, jingling them in my face. "You won't get very far without them."

I gave a grim chuckle. I noticed she had on a black leather jacket, like she was going somewhere. "Say, you couldn't drop me off at the church, could you? St Mary's?"

"Hop in then."

Maybe she'd been overcome with guilt, I thought as I drove towards her request stop. She didn't strike me as the religious sort, though anything was possible. The girl had foxed me from the off.

I pulled over outside the church. "There's a short cut through the churchyard," she said. "You couldn't walk with me – just to the other side? It gets a bit creepy this time of night."

I sighed as I turned off the engine and clambered out of the car. This would be my one last favour and then it would be curtains for Tiger Heart, I vowed. The churchyard was reasonably lit by the sodium-yellow of a bordering street lamp, filtered by wavering trees. When we'd passed through to the front side of the church she stopped dead in her tracks. "By the way you didn't tell me," she said. "You didn't tell me about your own headboard. You made a promise and you broke it."

I didn't say anything. My headboard was as my head: closed to anyone who thought they could move in on my ideas. She thought she could catch me off guard, but she couldn't.

"Well, that's a great shame," she said, walking backwards away from me and doing something weird with her fingers. "Because I know just how your next one will look." Then she stopped to grip a huge shiny headstone. We both looked at Tough Granite, then at each other. I looked away first, not able to hold her gaze. Then she disappeared into the shadows.

RECIPE FOR A SHORTENED TERM IN OFFICE

Cooking time: several weeks

For many servings

1 Politician
1 Politician's Wife
1 Lapdancer (preferable Swedish)
1 Source of Leak
1 Scoop of Tabloid Press

1 Piece of New Legislation on Family Values (prepared beforehand)
Politician's Children (Optional)

1) Place Politician and Lapdancer in compromised situation and combine. For added bite, make sure Politician is a reputable make and very mature. Lapdancer needs to be full-bodied and fresh.

2) Gradually introduce Politician's Wife, making sure to get the consistency right for a fuller flavour. It helps if Politician's Wife is mature, bland and malleable. This can be achieved by keeping Wife close to Politician over a number of years, allowing Wife to absorb some of Politician's flavour.

3) In a separate area, stir up Source of Leak and add Scoop of Tabloid Press.

4) To Tabloid Source, add New Legislation on Family Values, prepared several weeks beforehand. This is

especially effective if individual parts of the Legislation are broken up into bite-size chunks. Keep stirring. The mixture should be rich and juicy.

5) Turn on the heat.

6) Whip up the Politician Mixture with the Tabloid Mixture. The Politician's Children can be added at this point.

7) Turn up the heat.

8) Cook at a high temperature for several weeks. It's normal for the resulting bake to crumble at the centre.

9) Serve with relish.

NB You can alter ingredients to suit personal taste eg try an Archbishop in place of the Politician. I have also found that a Fresh Male Model works just as well in place of the Lapdancer. The Children are optional but they add a bit more bite. For a more hot and spicy flavour, try substituting a Moroccan Lapdancer for the Swede.

THE SUIT

He has become his suit. Few can resist the role the suit demands.   You can become any set of clothes. Sometimes they are bigger than you.

The weather is fine this morning but he takes his umbrella anyway, it's like a third leg as he strides past the post box. The small one in the wall where you post little white letters, like bills. Where girls write to their friends in frilly pink envelopes. Where doomed job applications get twisted and caught on the wire braces. He uses the stand-alone one on the corner of Dunster Avenue for his important mail. His A4 manilla envelopes, too macho for the puny mouth in the wall. The Dunster Avenue one is a proper pillar box, big and meaty. Wide, open-mouthed, you hear your letters being swallowed whole, not just a delicate tickle in the back of the throat. The Dunster Avenue box is where he posted off his successful job application. The job which led to the Suit.

At the train station, he queues at the ticket office. He can smell last night's onion on the breath of the man behind him as he checks the clock on the wall. The woman in front of him can sense his impatience. She makes way for the Suit. "You go ahead of me," she says. "I've got twenty minutes before my train." He pays by plastic, his card and ticket are swivelled round to him. On the platform, passengers watch as the digital clock clicks on the minutes. Those with cases shuffle closer to the edge to be first on the train. He buys the Daily Telegraph and a cup of coffee with a lid. You have to buy a paper to match the Suit.

On the train he sits in one of those few seats in a

confrontational arrangement, with a table. Most of the other seats are packed in rows, like on buses. He should really be in First Class. Opposite him is an older man, leaning his elbows on his brief case which stands on his knees. His small son's brightly-coloured lunch box is similarly placed on his own small knees. The father's suit is grey, his shoes huge and black with lots of polish and few creases. There's a lot to this suit business. His own is navy blue. He brushes a few specks off his lapel and looks at his paper. The train judders into action. He hears threads of conversation cutting across his snatched reading about the state of the NHS. 4 Across is blank blank T blank blank. What time will we arrive at– ? He folds his newspaper and pops open his briefcase.

"Is this seat taken?"

He shifts his open briefcase onto the table so the young girl can sit down next to him. In the corner of his eye, he can see her crossed denimed leg swinging in time to the hiss on her ipod. The typed documents feel important in his hands. But it's full of errors. Why do so many people put an apostrophe in 'its' or anything ending in an 's', to that matter, where there clearly shouldn't be one? He gives furtive glances over his neighbour's shoulder every so often, to see the kind of book she's reading. To see if there's any juicy sex. He catches a line. *I love men in uniform, says Judy.* A woman's book. A mobile phone rings. His. It's Leonie. She's going to be late again she says. She's recovering from one of her migraines. He shakes his head.

At work, he feels the tone change as he enters the office. Sort of deferential. It's the Suit. Mary Potts makes him some coffee. She wears a suit too. A cream suit. But it doesn't have the same effect. Not here anyway. Because she's too old now to climb the corporate ladder. "How many spoons of White Death would you like today?" she asks. "Three," he says. The Suit gives him a sweet tooth. The White Death and the lunchtime beers are giving him a slight paunch under his vest under his white shirt.

He chairs the meeting this morning. Leonie flusters in during Apologies, clutching her head. She's yawning by Matters Arising and positively nodding off by Correspondence. Mary Potts has to elbow her awake in Any Other Business.

In the middle of the day, after a hard morning's work, he wanders across the road to the sandwich bar which caters for Suits like his. He looks like an executive on his lunch hour. Few concessions to the warm weather except his jacket is still in his office around the back of his leather chair which swivels. Whenever he sits in it, he becomes that important chair. He hurries back with his heart-attack sandwich, no time for beer today.

His diary is on his desk along with the picture of his fiancée and the pot plant. He used to know about different plants. He used to water them. Now he leaves that to Mary Potts. He looks at his watch. He's insecure if he doesn't know the time. He picks up the phone. "Mary? Can you tell Leonie I'd like to see her in my office, please?"

"Sit down, please." He gestures to the smaller leather chair, the one on the other side of the table which doesn't swivel. He flips up the top page of a two-page report which is paper-clipped together, giving a fleeting glance at the under page.

"Well? It's happened again, hasn't it?"

"I'm sorry," says Leonie. "But I felt really awful this morning. I think I've got a bit of a virus."

He frowns. He can't afford the inconvenience of illness and so he never is ill. He assumes other people are ill because they want to be.

"I did try and get in as soon as I could," she says. "It won't happen again."

"How many times have I heard that?" He spins his gold pen in his hands. "I'm sorry but you've had your last warning." It's the Suit talking. "We're going to have to let you go."

"Let me go?"

"Correct." He looks down. He's finished dealing with her. He's surprised to find her still there when he looks up. "You can collect your P45 from personnel on your way out."

He feels a slight irritation as she makes her way to the door, her leather duffle bag gaping open-mouthed. Watched, she trips a bit on the carpet as she reaches for the handle. The door closes behind her. He rocks back in his chair, hands behind his head, and blows out. Not so difficult, though his face feels red. But it'll get easier. The Suit will see to that. He looks at his watch. There's never enough time in the day when you're wearing the Suit.

"Nice day at the office?" his fiancée asks when he gets home.

"Usual," he says, through a satisfying fatigue. "I'll go and run a bath,"

"You won't be long, will you? I'm going out in twenty."

Upstairs, he feels the power draining from him as he takes off the suit and hangs it up. He briefly catches sight of his flesh in the mirror: pale and defenceless without its armour. In the bath he tries to recapture the feeling the suit gives him. Did he really fire Leonie? But in the suit he's the office king.

He hears his fiancée rapping on the door. "Come on, hurry up in there. I need to spray my hair." There's a definite change to her tone. "And don't leave the bath a scummy mess."

Obediently he hoicks out the plug and calls over the snoring bathwater. "Where is it you're going again?"

She tuts. "Another interview. I did tell you."

"Oh good luck."

But as she swings into the bathroom he realizes she won't need luck. Her double-breasted red suit, starched so stiff you wouldn't want to cross it, will surely outperform its rivals.

She applies the finishing touches to her appearance and leaves the bathroom with a note of authority.

She is becoming her suit. Few can resist the role the suit demands. Sometimes it is bigger than you.

THE COLOUR OF FLESH

All started when I says to my mate Rick, don't laugh but I'm getting an accent. Just like that. I'm sick of being a kid with no voice. Kids with accents, with voices, they sound stronger like, innit? I never said it like that then. Thought about the accent thing a bit. North or south? This country even? Then Rick switches on the telly, hittin me with ideas. "The first strong one I hear, Ricko, that'll be it."

I knows it, sister, anyway. Before the voice and the kid comes up on TV, I get this feelin, always had it, deep down in here, innit? See I might look white with my blond hair and pale skin, but I'm black inside. Don't no nothin about no black culture, not even black music, though I'm trying to do garage and hip hop like and rap, it's a feelin I get in me when I'm hearin it, an I'm smokin the weed which I'm callin ganja, an I might be messin up, making mistakes, big time, but it's the tone I respec see, it's the tone an the voice, more than gettin it right. It's the tone what gives me the confidence, an I want the confidence, right, when I arks Jasmine out. She's the best-lookin black kid at our white school. She don't have no hot black boy sniffin round an I can be the next best thing, innit? She's here, right here with her white mate, two bus seats in front of me and Rick as we're ridin home. Don't laugh at me if I fuck it up but she's real cute, she gotta a cute ass, real cheeky smile. Jasmine sounds a real sweet-smellin name, intoxifyin, like night perfume. There was this black woman called Blossom, there's this white flower thing goin on, don't arks me, I don't know shit.

Rick keeps windin me. "You gonna wimp out on me, Benjie boy?"

"Don't give me no shit, man. An it's Leroy. The name is Leroy, right."

"We gotta bet on, *Leroy*." (Rick talks like me sometimes, with the voice, caught off me.) "Five pound says she freezes you out."

"Hey listen up," I says, an now my Jasmine is swishin that sweet ass of hers across that hot padded leather, she's dingin the bell, she's dingin all the bells, the one on the bus, and the ones in my pants, this ain't no cakewalk, you wanna hear me heart, my other ole love organ, bangin that African drum, innit?

"Bet you don't get as far as asking her."

No? See I'm turnin round at him with my finger pointing right at him. A friendly sorta shooter. Like I'm sayin to him in my head, you don't win no bets with Leroy see. You can have em but you aint winnin em.

But now I'm followin Jasmine, I got the confidence when I got the voice, an I want the black girl, I wanna her bad, an she's fizzin off the bus like a firework, her an her white mate an all and I'm sniffin along behind them, like a bitch on heat, yeah, you got my number innit, an I never heard no talk from her, I never heard what she even sounded like, an Rick is bangin the bus window half way to Torquay. Ain't sure of the voice no more, an she might mow me down, Jasmine, her with her cute ass an I'm right up behind her, all the little braids criss-crossin her head, flat against, not like my skanked up dreads. Loops of gold in her ears, gotta be 24 carat, real quality.

An I'm waitin for the white mate to shoot off down her nice white road with the nice pussy-willow an all coz me and Jasmine got other stuff to sort out, boy girl stuff. Come on, sister, me an the party girl don't wanna talk no biology homework, not from no books, you get me?

"Hey, Jazz, come back to mine," says White Mate. "Let's do our homework together."

Jazz, hey. That's cool. That's hot. That's my party chick.

Got arks her before all the confidence is gone, know what I mean? I'm steppin in next to em, Jazz and her mate, doin my cool walk, beefin up the rhythm, like I'm dancin already, steppin out now in front of Jazz, like on the dance floor.

"You commin out Saturday, yeah?" Don't want her mowin me down, so I'm speakin in the space. "Fancy checkin out that new club The Station?"

White Mate is splittin her face. "Go on, Jazz. Make his day."

"OK."

"Meet you outside about nine, yeah?"

"OK."

OK. Two lots OK! An a sassy smile to show me her pukka teeth! Fuck man, I'm flyin. We're on a date Saturday night, I'm winnin me bet, an shit, I should be takin the lady for a drink first, innit, my brain is gone putty, coz we're on a date Saturday no shit!

My mum, she's got my measure, I'm comin in, right, like I'm the daddy, yeah the big daddy of um all coz of my hot date Saturday.

"Is it a girl, Ben?" my mum arks.

She never calls me Leroy, though I told her. Ben is the name you was born with. She don't quite say it like that, only in my head. In my head, she is black mama cookin me Jamaican food with the best rum and spices and sweet potato, that's what I'm smellin instead of that bland white cheese junk in the pan.

"It is a girl, isn't it? What's she called?"

"Jasmine." I'm whistlin and pickin the bland junk from off the wood spoon which I'm spicin up in my head.

"She is call Jasmine."

"Nice."

"She's real quality. Gotta date Saturday."

"Nice."

She means it, my mum, she wants me to do happy, I'm all she's got. I'm the daddy, an I'm woofin down the blan cheez junk, on my life, coz after tomorrow is Saturday innit, an I gotta work up, do the spadework, start sprucin myself, know what I mean?

My mama is goin off out to her singin class tonight, I went with her for the taster in Week One when she told me the songs was cross-culture. I thought some of my black brothers and sisters will check it out for sure but there was only these Sheilas and these Pennys right, fifty right, white as meringue, yeah? This is Devon we're talkin, this ain no meltin pot. I wish there was more black kids round here to learn off instead of off the telly, I don't do much telly coz the African in me likes to keep moving my feet, it's the rhythm in me, the soul. I wanna be like the black street kids, don't read me wrong, sister, I ain't talkin no knives in my boot, shit like that, I'm talkin graffiti and warehouses and roots reggae. But at this class, there ain't none of that, all white as meringue, no kids my own age. There was this song we done, went somethin like ambassa dower amma dower dower tooay tooay, dunno what it's sayin, don't wanna know, it's the mystery innit, the power you get under your ribs when you're singin them words from far-off, down deep, power of unity, one voice. I'm talkin spirit, stuff that shakes you, know what I mean, like songs do, the black songs, ain talkin no heavy Jesus stuff, but it makes you high singin them words, with the power in your ribcage. Makes you buzz some.

So now my mama is off at her class singin that song again, an I'm singin it too lookin in my mirror, screwin up my eyes, seein the African in me, or the West Indian, I don't know fuck which. Jamaica. Trinidad & Tobago. Yeah, I been in one of them places in my former lives, you just know it. Shit, Hackney is exotic to the Devon crew, know what I'm sayin? So I'm screwin up my eyes till the hair is gone black yeah, black and tight, an my skin's glowin, startin off gold, 24 carat, like Jasmine's earrin, like West Indian, an gettin darker, till all I'm seein is dark damson, a class colour. Black as Africa. Yeah. I'm seein my dark eyes like I want Jasmine to see them when we have our big date Saturday. I'm starin in on my black self, keepin it there, lockin it into me right, till I can't do no more lockin, an then I'm decidin to do a bit of cleanin up and stuff coz mama is out singin it some, singin ambassa dower. I'm goin into her room, lookin for a thing to dust with and I am seein this brand new pair of tights, still in their packet. But it's what it says on the packet. *30 denier. Flesh-coloured.*

"Fuck, that might be the colour of yours, sista, but mine's this colour. Black. Dark damson black, you get me?"

"What's that, Ben?"

Well spooky innit, my mama back already.

"Leroy!" How many times did I arks her call me Leroy? "Sing the song?"

"Not that one, no, but we did *Shame and Scandal.*"

She singin it now, all about Antigua and a family with much confusion as you will see, there was a mama and a papa an a boy who was grown, an this boy wanted to get married have a wife of his own, he meets a girl, she treated him nice, goes to his papa to ask his advice, his papa says son I have to say no, that girl is your sister but your mama don't know. She shows me the song sheet with all this black humour incest stuff goin on, it's in *sane*, bro.

"I remember that song," my mama's sayin.

See now I know my mama is black deep down too, an I'm pullin out the little Philips' Pocket Atlas of the World, lookin up Antigua, coz somewhere like it was my home once, you gotta check out your homeland, an now I'm placin it, I'm on the West Indies page, an I'm seein Trinidad an Jamaica, an I'm hearin all the music, seein all the colour, the dancin, feelin all the hot sun from my homeland, an I'm feelin homesick yeah? All them little islands faraway in the Caribbean Sea but I'm havin a date with Jasmine Saturday – a taste of home, know what I mean?

I don't see no Torbay Sea walkin the walk this Saturday night, not even no Caribbean Sea, I'm seein docks an big warehouses where we're goin clubbin, heart of London, I'm out on the street, meetin my date in this big city, yeah, along with the rest of the crew, I can hear the rappin, smell the spices, feel the danger coz I'm a bit different right, my heart goin calypso crazy. It's nine, it's fine, out on the street, to meet, outside the club, an all the hub, what if she don't show, I'll have to go, an cry, ain got no time to cry, ain got no time to die–

Fuck man, here she commin! She commin over, short slinky number, white as stars. She is a star! I'm kitted up real neat, bit blingy in my rings an stuff but you gotta look the part, dress to impress, hair with the gel an stuff, right?

I givin it a bit of rhythm, spinnin round, then I'm pointing the finger at her, the friendly shooter an I'm sayin, "Sassy baby!"

I'm all bug-eyed walkin in The Station with my Jasmine, white dress clingin on her like a swimsuit. Smart place, big station clock over the bar, yeah, an big signs, black on white, sayin STATION BAR an WAITING ROOM an there's the WAGONS all round the side to sit in, drinkin your drinks, an the people workin here is wearin the gear, like you get on a proper train, innit? An that big red signal pointin upwards over the dance floor, it's well sick.

"You go sit in one of them wagons, Jazz, can I call you Jazz, it's sorta cool, an I'll get us in the hooch." I'm hearin the shake in my black voice, like I'm gonna lose it, like I'm goin off the station, know what I mean? "Woss your poison, Jazz?"

"Can I have a glass of chilled white wine?"

On my life I had this vision of her drinkin something dark, something with coke, rum and coke, right, or Tia Maria and coke, or Black Russian, an me bringin it to her with the ice an all, the little umbrella, yeah? You know what I'm sayin, an I'm gettin myself one of these anyway right, an I'm sittin face on face with her in the wagon, it's makin the jungle drum beat in me, no kiddin, an there's the two mega train signals side of the dance floor an kids up there steppin on it, an I'm sayin, "let's go out there, Jazz, do our stuff," coz I been dreamin of us up there doin sassy.

The drink is loosenin me an I'm takin hole her hand, feels stiff, she don't look like no shy babe. I'm gettin this picture of her, dead centre of the floor, an their playin brown girl in the ring, she look like a sugar in a plum, an she's a real party diva in the ring, widder little teats showin thru her tight bathing-dress, but my Jazz is doin shy.

"I'm not getting up there."

"Come on, give me sassy, Jazz."

But she slips out my hand an she's headin off the train, sista, she's headin right out the station, an I'm goin after her, next stop the beach.

"Hey, give me a line, Jazz."

She's frownin up her sweet face. "Why d'you keep

talking in that funny way?"

Funny way? That hurts, on my life, piercin my ole love organ.

"I shouldn't have come out tonight. I hate nightclubs."
"Hate nightclubs? But there's all that dancin an stuff."
"I hate dancing. I *can't* dance."
"Can't dance?" She is stunnin the words right out of me, on my life.

"I know I know. I'm black. We're supposed to be able to dance."

She is sittin down on the sand, combin her fingers through it.

"Come and sit by me, Ben. I want to let you into a secret."

And this is what she sayin. She sayin: It all started when I was sitting by my friend at school, Elise, and I had this picture in my head, just like that. A picture of a nineteen-fifties girl. She was like an ice-cream with her blond hair stacked up on top, and her tanned body like a cone, and her lips pink like raspberry ripple. Well, I might look like any other black kid my age on the outside but I'm Miss Whippee on the inside. It's a feeling I get when I see those nineteen-fifties blondes in their bright swimming costumes. I want to be like them. That's where my fantasy takes me on the dreary bus home. When I heard your mate, Rick, cutting into my daydreams with "Five pounds says she freezes you out," I liked that talk of freezing, Ben. I thought you guys must see me as cold. That's a good start for Miss Whippee! So as I'm climbing out of the seat I do a sexy move – like Marilyn Munroe. I can hear you clambering off the bus behind me, but I am only thinking about my hair, maybe dying it blonde, maybe stacking it up on top, like a scoop of Wall's, and then sticking a dark brown slide in it, like a milk flake, and that'll be my only concession to chocolate. Then you came up behind me and asked me out.

When I get home my mum says, "Is it a boy, Jazz?" And that's another thing. I wish people would stop calling me Jazz. It sounds so black and bluesy. Put 'min' on the end and you've got something white and creamy. Nearly minty. Mint ice-cream! Up in my bedroom, I'm working on my pout. I'm screwing up my eyes, imagining false spidery lashes batting down over smouldering eyes. If I try, try hard, I see the Miss Whippee in me. I see my hair whipped up to a creamy point, a slide holding it together, like a 99. I must have been a Butlins Red Coat in another life, like in *Hi De Hi*. I must have gone for two weeks holiday in Scarborough or Blackpool with my shift dress tapering into my golden legs like a cone. Boys and men must have said I looked good enough to eat. Where are the ice-cream girls now, Ben? Anyway, I slip this old stocking of my mum's over my head and face. My spotlight is shining off the mirror, it's dazzling, and I can see the swirl of cream that is my hair and I'm shaking it, it's melting over my shoulders, down the gold skin of my body. All I'm seeing is Miss Whippee and blobs of raspberry sprinkled over my pale cheeks. Next thing, my mum comes into my room saying, "I've lost one of my stockings – you seen it, Jazz?"

"What colour?"

"They're flesh-coloured."

She meant light flesh, of course.

Then she screams when she sees me – she wasn't looking before. "Christ, you look like a hoodlum with that over your head, squashing your features like that!" I pull the stocking off my head. "My stockings! They're ruined, Jazz. This one's too baggy even for *my* legs." She snatches it off me. "What were you doing anyway? Are you practising something for your drama?"

In a way, I think.

And, well – you know the rest, Ben, but it was too hot in that club. I thought I'd end up an oozy mess on the dance floor.

An now I'm tranna kiss her, that comes next, innit, an our lips touch, I feel the ice cool of her tongue in mine, an I chokin, my voice is got stuck in my throat, like a lump of ice. She's bangin my back and then it comes out. We both see it land in the sand, like a set of false teeth or something embarrassing. It looks revolting, and a bit plastic. We peer at it, before I scuff some sand over it. I don't know how she did it but I reckon she cut it loose with the icy edge of her tongue.

One thing's for sure, she did me a favour.

Years later, she tells me she only meant for it to melt, but I learned my lesson anyway.

A GENERATION THING

She's nineteen, birth date: June 6th 1984. Her mum and dad were born in the fifties when the car was still a rarity and Bournemouth was still in Hampshire. She was born in Bournemouth, the posh part, not all Bournemouth's posh, though people from the north say it is. Her dad's from the north, somewhere called Redcar, though the only place she's been in the north is Warwick, somewhere like that beginning with a W.

Her boyfriend was born in Poole. She asked her boyfriend out. (Whoever made it that boys do the asking when it's girls that have the communication skills?) She doesn't question the idea of equality between boys and girls as her mother did: it's taken as red, isn't it? If she can be a prick tease, he can be a clit tease, end of. She knows what she wants and how to get it. Should I go on top? Can we try spoons? Her mum envies her. When her mum was her age spoons were pieces of cutlery you used for dessert. She pays her way, and more often than not, her boyfriend's, seeing how he's always skint. When her mum was her age, it was a big thing to go Dutch. She thought her mum was talking about a holiday in Amsterdam. Her mum had some wild times though. She fancied the lead singer of Mud – Les someone or other? – and threw her knickers at him at a pop concert. They missed and got the curly girlie one instead. They were posh knickers, trimmed in pink lace, size 34 hip, from a shop called Etam's. (Thongs weren't invented). Unlike her mum, she's never been to a pop concert. She was going to do Glastonbury last year, it was her friend's idea, but they didn't get round to it. Plus it does her head in the way her parents think they invented Glastonbury. She wonders if people will look back on Popstars, The Rivals, in the same way as her mum and dad look back on The Seventies. Her dad said they were manufactured, the Popstars. Not like in our day, he said. Not like David Bowie. Her dad likes David Bowie. So does she. It's not right, kids liking the same music as their folks, wasn't the same in our day, her dad says. Yeah right, and what about parents liking the same as their kids, her brother says when her dad borrows her Strokes CD (though her dad says The Strokes would lend themselves to the superior sound of vinyl rather than CD). Her brother doesn't do The Seventies. Her brother likes Eminem. Her brother is original Gadget Boy. He texts his mates to tell them he's breathing, walking, crapping even. *Call u in 5 wen dun No 2.* We only had a party line when we were growing up, her dad says. Her brother looks at him like he's winding him up. Surely they couldn't have had chat lines that long ago? Her brother is in Year 11. Her dad still calls it the fifth year. Just to make a point. We still have classrooms, dad, her brother says. And double maths. And teachers. Hey chill out, her dad says to her brother (thinking he's Well Funky, instead of So Nineties).

But if she says the funky word to her dad, he'll say it was around in his day. He so wants it both ways. He wants everyone to know that what comes around has gone around. He also wants it known that what comes around was never around in his day. For example, discos were around in his day, but drinking out of bottles wasn't. The done thing was to drink out of glasses which were sometimes plastic because his generation were an angry passionate lot who weren't to be trusted with a pint glass (until he sees the latest crime figures for the region, and then it's back to Those Were The Days when you could walk the streets in safety.)

Teenage rebellion is his biggest beef. He did it, they haven't. Except for a few Roads Protesters and that's going back a few years. (Too right). Nowadays, even fairweather protesters are thin on the ground, he says. I suppose it's not your fault that you're part of the dumbed-down, post-Blair, global years. (Dad, what are you like?) His other hobby horse is student protest, or lack of. She and her boyfriend are students at Bournemouth University, though her dad still calls it The Wally Poly, (Wally because it's based at Wallisdown). Unis were unis back then, he says, and kids your age left home to rebel and march for higher grants. He is surely living in la-la land. All that happy hippy stuff is done and dusted. She so doesn't want to change the world. She wants to get on. Be something. She doesn't wannabe a wannabe. She and her boyfriend have this motto: *Work Hard Shag Hard.* They thought it up in the student library last week. Her dad says there is more to life than the Work Ethic and there should be time to stand and stare (at what?) Standing still equals stagnation in her books. Her mum is right with her on this one. Her mum is doing a TEFL course. (That's Teaching English as a Foreign Language, her mum explained for the benefit of her brother whose ears prick every time he hears a new set of initials, in case they refer to a new gadget). Language and international communication are the way forward, her mum says. Her mum has done lots of courses as a mature student. Her mum says it keeps her young but makes her feel old when she sees all These Young Things. She tells her mum to get into the Botox groove in that case. Two of her friends' mums have done it. She will try it herself when she's twenty-nine, or when her first crow's-feet appear, whichever comes first. She swears she'll be doing it for herself only, though her mum says it's always done with a man in mind. It doesn't really matter why: she doesn't want to look like a minger around people who've had face jobs. She wants to be able to pull when she's thirty, in case she needs to, because men don't come with a ten-year loyalty sticker these days. Neither do girls. It's all musical beds from here on in. (Bring it on!)

How sad is that, her mum says (trying to sound funky like her dad).

Those were the days when you didn't give your cherry to anyone, her mum says.

Those were the days when sex was still sexy, her dad says.

Though she knows those weren't the days. These are.
(And always are).

BISCUITS

- Kit, 1968 -

No account of a sixties childhood is complete without a mention of the biscuits. A biscuit for every occasion. As a boy I liked to grade them: fancy, medium and plain. Except those broken biscuits from Reece's which defied classification – the once-aspiring, rubbing shoulders with the workaday. Wilma and I would stop outside the window in Reece's and see the fragmented displays in the tilted plastic jars with their side openings. We'd pay our pennies and come away each with a cone of greaseproof paper full of biscuit chippings, drooling as we walked and munched. Eating in the street was frowned upon in those days, but we literally couldn't wait to get them back to our respective homes which would mean sneaking them past the adults.

In Aunt Lil's scratched flowery tin, the one that you had to hold to your chest while gripping the underside of the lid with your nails to wrench it off, the assortment was always plain. Rich Tea. Lincoln with the bobbles. Nice. Digestives. Royal Scott with the big fluted edges and criss-crosses on the back. Now and again, the biscuits would verge on the bottom end of medium – Abbey Crunch, ginger nuts. Occasionally Aunt Lil would have in these posh Barmouth biscuits, slightly caramelled and shiny with a dark brown, rough edge – crunchy in comparison to the gone-soft plains. *Fancy biscuits will spoil your teeth, Kit.*

For some reason I associated the biscuits with church. Not tea and biscuits in the vestry with the adults after

Sunday school, but going from house to house on a sort of biscuit crawl where I expected the class of biscuit to elevate or descend according to the class of the host, though sometimes you were fooled.

Wilma's mother had recently become High Church and for the prospect of the biscuit crawl afterwards, I would sometimes accompany Wilma to Sunday school, the content of which I can scarcely recollect. In contrast, the biscuits remain sharp, twinkling with sugar and colour. I wasn't sure what High Church involved exactly, only that it must be superior in some way to ordinary church if the biscuits at Wilma's were anything to go by. They were as colourful as her mother's black skin with its areas of plum and bronze and pink. In Primrose's tin could be found all the top-of-the-range favourites. Chocolate fingers, marshmallows, lemon puffs, iced biscuits with coffee or white you could suck off. I daresay Primrose kept a tin of plains somewhere in her kitchen, but even her plains would border on the medium, I suspected. Coconut Rings, Garibaldis, shortbreads, that sort of thing. A hint of flavour was always in evidence in the Phillips' household.

Our next port of call was usually the Dearloves over the road at Number 28 – that was, if Wilma and Gillian were friends that week. They were always making and breaking friends, it was hard to keep up. On the rooves of the houses along the road stood an assortment of old H aerials, same shape as the rugby stands in the rugby football ground further along the Liverpool Road. This was pre-1969 and the Dearlove television was just the same as Aunt Lil's, taking about five minutes or more to warm up. You could watch the orange valves lighting up through the holes in the back of the telly that went on for miles. While waiting for the telly to stir itself to life, we'd pack in another couple of biscuits, this time from the

Dearlove tin. The Dearlove biscuits were a bit of a comedown after Wilma's, but still not to be sniffed at. A custard cream. A Bourbon. Biscuits with layers. Biscuits you could take apart. Medium biscuits. "Oh it's a bugger of a thing," Gillian's dad could be heard saying on the Dearlove party line and Mrs Dearlove would reprimand him for swearing on a Sunday. They were only occasional church-goers as far as I knew – of the Protestant variety.

We left Gillian before making our way to our final destination in the road: the Dackies at Number 7. I expected bickies at the Dackies to be the cheapest plainest things or non-existent. That may have been the case in Terry's ma's tin at the high rise in Kirkby, but at Number 7 his grandma splashed out on a few luxuries. Pink and chocolate wafers and jammy dodgers twinkled between the bog-standard Marie biscuits which you had to poke aside, like you did with your more boring marbles to get at the rarer species hiding beneath, leaving the Plains for Grandpa Dackie to dunk in his tea, though his usual poison was coloured black and came in a bottle, accompanied by a Woodie rather than a bickie. They were fresh from Mass, the grandparents, and whichever of the Dacosta lads – Terry, Jackie, Chas and Joey, and their sister Mo – were over from Kirkby. The telly would be on in the parlour but you couldn't hear it above the raucous Scouse squabbles. One time a couple of their Irish cousins, the Mulcahys, were round there. Billy and Shane Mulcahy. Only they didn't sound Irish. It was their ma and da that were from Derry originally, along with Terry's ma. They were Evertonians, Toffees, whereas the Dackies were fierce Reds causing much baiting and backbiting over the bickies. Though mostly it was the bickies themselves causing the contention. *Array. He's took the last fuckin chocky one. No I fuckin never.* "Holy mother of Mary." Grandma Dackie was no pushover. "Mind your language, you lads, or you'll get a battering." Though it was difficult for the lads to learn by example. Not with the effing and blinding that ensued from Grandpa Dackie's mouth after a few Guinnesses, Sunday or not.

Shane Mulcahy, the younger of the Mulcahy boys, openly gloated, the chocolaty pulp of his biscuit being churned on his tongue for all who cared to watch. "Gob shut, gobshite." Grandpa Dackie was thrifty with the f words for once.

It was time to go home to our respective roast dinners. As I said goodbye to Wilma outside Number 23, I thought how we needed to change the route so we could end up at Wilma's. That way we could save the best biscuits till last.

Aunt Lil's wasn't on the itinerary, of course. Her biscuits, so seldom dispatched, were too soft, even for a hungry Dacosta lad. I returned to Number 37 and the smell of Yorkshire Pudding. "Did you have a nice time at Wilma's after Sunday School?" she said. "Now I hope you haven't eaten anything, Kit, that might spoil your appetite." I looked at her like butter wouldn't melt, let alone a chocolate digestive.

I was a growing lad and biscuits in all shapes and styles were my horses d'oovrers before the Sunday roast.

#####

About the author:

Kate Rigby was born in Crosby, Liverpool and now lives in Devon. She studied Psychology at Southampton, though she's given up paid work on health grounds. She's written 15 books and many of her short stories have been published or shortlisted. She's been writing novels for over thirty years now. She loves cats, singing, music, photography and LFC.

Further details about Kate's work can be found at her website:

http://kjrbooks.yolasite.com/

Her occasional blogs can be found at:

http://bubbitybooks.blogspot.com/

Printed in Great Britain
by Amazon